# ANASTASIA
# AT YOUR
# SERVICE

OTHER YEARLING BOOKS BY LOIS LOWRY YOU WILL ENJOY:

YEARLING BOOKS/YOUNG YEARLINGS/YEARLING CLASSICS are designed especially to entertain and enlighten young people. Patricia Reilly Giff, consultant to this series, received her bachelor's degree from Marymount College and a master's degree in history from St. John's University. She holds a Professional Diploma in Reading and a Doctorate of Humane Letters from Hofstra University. She was a teacher and reading consultant for many years, and is the author of numerous books for young readers.

For a complete listing of all Yearling titles, write to Dell Readers Service, P.O. Box 1045, South Holland, IL 60473.

# ANASTASIA AT YOUR SERVICE

## LOIS LOWRY

Decorations by Diane de Groat

A YEARLING BOOK

Published by
Bantam Doubleday Dell Books for Young Readers
a division of
Bantam Doubleday Dell Publishing Group, Inc.
1540 Broadway
New York, New York 10036

ISBN: 0-440-40290-5

Reprinted by arrangement with Houghton Mifflin Company

Printed in the United States of America

One Previous Edition

August 1992

20   19

OPM

*For Ben and Grey*

# ANASTASIA AT YOUR SERVICE

# 1

"Groan," said Anastasia Krupnik feebly, and kicked the living room couch with one sneaker. She was lying on the living room floor. She was terribly depressed. She was so depressed that she had been acting out all the deathbed scenes she could think of. Beth, in *Little Women*. (A few small coughs, and then, weakly, "Farewell, my dear sisters.")

Juliet. (A gulp of poison, a horrible face because poison probably tasted terrible, and then, sadly, "Sorry things didn't work out, Romeo.")

Charlotte, in *Charlotte's Web*. (No final words, because spiders couldn't talk. But a few writhes. Probably spiders would writhe, dying. Then all eight legs — or six? Anastasia couldn't remember — straight up in the air.

Tough to act that one out, when you had only two legs.)

She wondered what would happen if her parents found her dead on the living room floor. Probably her mother would say, "For Pete's sake, I just cleaned this room yesterday, and *now* look at it."

She groaned again. "Groan." Feebly, still, but a little louder.

There was no response from anywhere. Deathbed scenes weren't any fun at all without an audience.

"GROAN," she roared, finally.

Her mother appeared in the doorway with an orange potholder mitten on one hand.

"Did you call me?" she asked cheerfully. "I thought I heard someone call 'Mom.'"

"I was groaning, for Pete's sake," said Anastasia. "Can't you even recognize a groan when you hear one?"

"Do it again."

"GROAN," roared Anastasia. Then she went on, dramatically, "I am dying. I have clasped an asp to my bosom."

"Must have been a heck of a disappointment for the asp. You hardly even *have* a bosom."

"*Mom!*" Anastasia sat up and threw a cushion at her mother.

"Sorry. That *was* a rotten thing to say. You've got the groaning wrong, though, incidentally. You don't *say* 'groan' when you're groaning. A good groan sounds like this: 'Arrgghh.'"

"Hey, that's pretty good."

"You try it."

2

"Arrggghhhh."

"Not bad. I would have come right away if I'd heard that. Do it again, louder."

"Aaarrrrgggghhhhh."

"Terrific. Wait a minute while I get my cup of coffee and then I'll ask you what's wrong."

Anastasia followed her mother to the kitchen and poured herself a glass of Kool-Aid.

"Now then," said her mother as she stirred her coffee, "what seems to be the problem?"

"Severe depression." Anastasia sighed.

"Well, I can *see* that. What's causing the depression?"

Anastasia thought, while she sipped her Kool-Aid. "Boredom," she said. "And also poverty. Extreme poverty."

"I can relate to that," said her mother. "At least to the poverty part. Your dad and I have never been rich. We never *will* be rich. English professors don't make very much money, and he's always going to be an English professor, because he loves it. And I'm always going to be an artist, because that's what *I* love, and artists never make much money."

"Mom," said Anastasia patiently, "I'm not talking about that kind of poverty. I'm talking about twelve-year-old, extreme, desperate, two-dollar-a-week-allowance kind of poverty. If I really *did* want to kill myself with an asp, I wouldn't be able to, because I wouldn't be able to *afford* an asp."

"True," said her mother. "Asps don't come cheap in Massachusetts."

"And as for the boredom . . ."

"Yes. Tell me about the boredom. I can't remember ever being bored. Also, Anastasia, I can't remember *you* ever complaining of boredom before. Just last week you were in and out of the house all the time, with a million things to do. You were playing tennis every day, and you were off riding your bike, and when I wanted you to help with the dishes I could never *find* you. Now I can *always* find you, because you're always lying on the floor saying, 'Farewell, cruel world.' What's happened?"

"Steve Harvey." Anastasia sighed. "The only person I *know* in this town. At least the only person my age. My tennis partner. My bike-riding companion. My only *friend,* for Pete's sake."

"I'm your friend," said a very small voice. Anastasia's brother, Sam, padded into the kitchen, with his shoes untied, and climbed into a chair. "I want some Kool-Aid. I want my friend Anastasia to pour me some Kool-Aid, please," he said.

"Oh, for Pete's sake," said Anastasia. She poured some Kool-Aid into Sam's plastic clown cup. "Here. Don't spill it."

"You're right, Sam," said her mother, smoothing his curly hair. "You are Anastasia's very dear friend. But right now she's not talking about two-year-old friends. What's happened to you and Steve, Anastasia? Did you have a fight?"

"No, of course not. But he's the only person my age that I've met since we've moved here. And he was going to introduce me to other kids before school started. He

4

was going to have a big cookout at his house. He was going to have it next *week*, in fact . . ."

"And now he isn't?"

"Now, for Pete's sake, he's *gone* all of a sudden. Somebody called his father, some big-deal sports figure, and asked if Steve would like to go to a basketball camp in New Hampshire. They gave him a full scholarship, for Pete's sake. Nobody's ever offered me a full scholarship anywhere, except that time Dad offered to buy me a one-way ticket to reform school."

"He was only kidding, Anastasia."

"No, he wasn't. He was really mad."

"Well, yes, that's true, he *was* really mad . . ."

"Because I left his dumb Billie Holiday records on the radiator and melted them."

"But he didn't mean it about reform school."

"I know." Anastasia sighed. "Watch it, Sam. You're going to spill that if you're not real careful." Sam had picked up the pitcher of Kool-Aid and was pouring himself another cup.

"No I won't," said Sam sweetly. Then the pitcher slipped out of his hand. Grape Kool-Aid poured over the kitchen table and into Anastasia's lap. Her best jeans. Her favorite shirt. Purple. And sticky. And *cold*.

"Aarrrgggghhhh," said Anastasia.

Sam climbed out of his chair quickly. "I'm going out to play," he said. "I'm going to play in the yard." He scooted through the back door.

Her mother grabbed two towels and a sponge and began to mop the table.

5

"Aarrrgggghhhh," said Anastasia again, holding her purple, cold, sticky shirt away from her body.

"Sam," called her mother through the kitchen window to the back yard, "while you're out there, look around in the bushes, would you? See if you can find an asp for your sister!"

"Ha, ha," said Anastasia, dripping sarcasm along with Kool-Aid.

✽

Anastasia loved suppertime. Especially when they had lasagna, as they did tonight. Her mother was the best lasagna-maker in the whole world. If ever there were a National Lasagna Bake-Off Contest, her mother would win, she was quite certain.

She had told her mother that once. But her mother had made a terrible face, with her eyes crossed and her tongue sticking out. Apparently her mother didn't want to win a National Lasagna Bake-Off Contest. Anastasia could understand that. Probably the prize would be an apron or something.

Even when they didn't have lasagna, Anastasia loved suppertime, because the whole family, all four of them, were there, and they talked a lot. Often they talked about their problems, and it was absolutely amazing, Anastasia thought, how problems seemed less monumental if you talked about them while you ate lasagna. Or even pot roast, or tuna-fish casserole.

When she was older, and her spelling had improved a bit, Anastasia planned to write an article for the

*Journal of the American Psychiatric Association.* In it, she was going to tell all the psychiatrists in America that if they served dinner to their patients, preferably lasagna (though pot roast or tuna-fish casserole would be okay), their patients would be cured of all their problems much faster.

("Oh, Doctor," Anastasia imagined a psychiatric patient saying, "I see purple leopards lurking behind the furniture. I will commit suicide if they don't go away."

"Hmmmm," the doctor would say. "Would you like some grated cheese on your lasagna? Tell me more about the purple leopards."

"Leopards? Were we talking about leopards? Funny, I don't remember anything about purple leopards. I would like more salad, though. And would you pass the rolls, please?")

"Dad," asked Anastasia as they ate, "do you have your notebook with you?"

He looked surprised. "Of course I have my notebook. I *always* have my notebook with me. Every writer does. You never know, if you're a writer, when you might have to take notes on the human scene." He took his small leather-bound notebook out of his pocket.

"No kidding. What does that mean: notes on the human scene?" asked Anastasia.

He thought for a minute. "Well, I eavesdrop and observe people. Then I make notes about what I see and what I overhear. After a while, I use some of that stuff in poems."

That was fascinating to Anastasia. She had tried and tried to be a writer, but somehow she had never succeeded very well. Yet her father, when he was not busy being an English professor, was a pretty successful writer of poetry. She had never figured out just how he did it. And now it turned out to be so simple. Notes on the human scene.

"Read me some," she suggested.

He put down his fork and flipped through the pages of his little notebook. "Well," he said, "here's what I wrote just this morning. 'Sam looks like his mother when he sleeps.'"

Anastasia's mother smiled. Sam smiled.

"'They both sleep with their mouths open, and their bottoms sticking up in the air,'" he went on.

Anastasia's mother stopped smiling. "Myron!" she said. "If you *ever* use that in a poem, I will sue for divorce!"

Dr. Krupnik grinned. "Just observations," he explained. "Notes on the human scene. Why did you ask if I had my notebook, Anastasia?"

"Because I have a problem. You always seem to need your notebook when you help me solve my problems."

"True," said her father. "I'm a list-maker. Most problems can be solved by making lists." He uncapped his fountain pen.

"I have a problem too!" said Sam suddenly, in a stricken voice. "Make me a list, *quick!*"

Anastasia groaned. Sam was always interrupting her serious discussions.

8

"What's your problem, Sam?" she asked in a bored voice. If they didn't deal with his first, he would keep interrupting.

"A pea in my nose," he said, sounding frightened.

"You put a *pea* in your nose? Sam! Why on earth did you do *that?*"

"Sometimes it's not important to ask why, Anastasia," said her mother. She picked Sam up and carried him away to the bathroom. After a moment they were back.

"Operation Pea Removal successful," announced Mrs. Krupnik. "Sam, do not *ever* do that again. It is very dangerous to put anything into your nose."

"Also your ears," said Anastasia. "Don't ever put anything into your ears."

Sam sat there looking guilty. He didn't say anything. It was unusual for Sam not to say anything.

"Sam?" said Anastasia's father.

Sam didn't answer. He was looking down into his lap. A very guilty look.

"Sam? Do you have peas in your ears?"

Sam shook his head.

"What's wrong, then?"

"My bellybutton," Sam whispered.

His father leaned over and lifted Sam's little shirt. There was a pea, slightly squashed, stuck on Sam's bellybutton.

Sometimes it was very, very difficult to have a serious meal with Sam around.

"Now," said her father finally, with his pen poised over his notebook, "back to your problem, Anastasia.

Sam, you eat your dinner. No more fooling around."

Anastasia listed her problems once again, for her father, the way she had for her mother that afternoon. Boredom. Poverty. Depression.

Dr. Krupnik wrote Boredom, Poverty, Depression in his notebook. He drew a box around them. He drew arrows pointing to the box. He drew a small flower. He drew three squiggly lines in a row. Finally he wrote one word with a flourish, underlined it, and put an exclamation point at the end of the word.

"There you are," he said. "Easy solution."

Anastasia pushed her glass of milk to one side so that she could see what he had written.

"*Job!*" it said at the bottom of the page.

Anastasia groaned.

"That sounds easy to you, Dad," she pointed out patiently, "because you're forty-seven years old and you *have* a job. You have a job teaching English at Harvard. And Mom, *you* have a job doing illustrations for that textbook on photography . . ."

"It is *not* easy," said her mother. "I spent all morning trying to draw the inside of a diffusion enlarger. If you think that's *easy*, Anastasia . . ."

"I didn't mean that. Of course the work isn't easy. But it's easy for you to get a job because you went to art school and everything. You have qualifications. Twelve-year-old people don't have qualifications for anything. Nobody gives a job to a twelve-year-old person."

Her father turned to a fresh page in his notebook. "Now the list-making really starts," he said happily.

"What do you mean?"

"Start thinking of the kinds of things you'd like to do. Things you'd be good at. Things someone might need someone to do. Then you'll start your own business, providing those services."

"Not baby-sitting. I hate baby-sitting."

Sam gave her a dirty look.

"Well, maybe I wouldn't mind baby-sitting if it were with a really well-behaved baby. But don't put baby-sitting down. Not until the very end, in case I'm desperate."

"Okay. Baby-sitting goes last. What shall I put first?"

Anastasia thought for a minute. "Well," she said at last, "promise not to laugh?"

"Anastasia!" said her mother. "We *never* laugh at you."

That was true. It was one of the things she liked about her parents.

"Okay. Here goes. What I'd really like to do — and I'd be good at, too — is to be a companion to an old lady. A really rich old lady. Like in mystery books by Mary Roberts Rinehart. Those really rich old ladies hire young girls — maybe not twelve, but I could do it just as well as someone older — to hang around and help them out with stuff. Read their mail to them. Make tea for them. Maybe polish their diamond bracelets and stuff like that. Of course, in the books they have to help solve mysteries, and I don't suppose anyone in this town needs mysteries solved. But there are all sorts of things that I could do for a rich old lady."

"Does she have to be rich?" asked her mother. "There are certainly a lot of *poor* — or even just average — old ladies who could use someone to help them out."

"Yeah," Anastasia acknowledged. "I know. But Dad asked me what I really wanted to do. And I think I'd really like to work for a *rich* old lady. We can put poor ones and average ones down as a separate category."

Her father nodded. He was busily taking notes.

"Goodness," said her mother. "What if some wealthy old woman really hired you, Anastasia? Wouldn't you be nervous? What would you say when you knocked on the front door? What if a *butler* answered?"

"Well, I guess I'd just say, 'Here I am: Anastasia Krupnik, at your service!' "

Sam giggled. His mouth was full of peas. "Anastasia atcherservice!" he said.

Dr. Krupnik was still writing things down.

"Tell you what," he said after a minute as he tore the page with the notes out of his notebook. "Instead of making a whole list, let's concentrate on this one at first, since it's what you want to do most. You write up a sort of résumé . . ."

"What's a résumé?" asked Anastasia.

"All the reasons that you'd be good at the job. Your past experience that makes you qualified."

"But I don't have any past experience."

"Well, if you think about things you've done in the past, you'll think of things that have some relevance. You've made tea plenty of times, for example. Would you call Anastasia an expert at making tea, Katherine?"

"Sure," said Mrs. Krupnik. "When I had the flu last winter, she made me endless cups of tea. And there was only that one disastrous cup . . ."

"That was *Sam's* fault!" objected Anastasia. "I'm not going to take the blame for that! Sam put the goldfish in without my even knowing! He thought it would be funny. And it *wasn't*. Poor Frank Goldfish practically went into *shock*, for Pete's sake! It was lucky he didn't *die!*"

"It was lucky *I* didn't die from shock," said her mother. "I thought I was having some horrible kind of hallucination when I picked up the cup and Frank Goldfish was floating beside the lemon slice."

Sam scrambled down from his highchair and left the dining room with dignity. "Excuse me," he said, at the door. "I'm full."

"Anyway," muttered Anastasia, "that doesn't reflect on my tea-making. I'm not going to put that in my résumé. It still makes me mad to think about it. Someday I'm really going to clobber Sam."

"I know the feeling," said her mother. "Sometimes I want to myself. A pea in his nose, for heaven's sake. How in the world did I give birth to a child who puts a pea in his nose?"

"Or a goldfish in a cup of tea." Anastasia glowered. "*My* goldfish."

"And remember that awful time he . . ." began her mother.

"Come on, ladies," said Dr. Krupnik. "That's all beside the point. You put your qualifications down, Anastasia, after you think of them. Then write a job description."

"What's that?"

"All the things you want to do in this job. You already listed some of them. Then put down your fees. And your phone number. Then I'll Xerox it for you at the office, and we'll figure out how to distribute the copies in places where rich old ladies might see them."

"That's easy," said Mrs. Krupnik. "There's a bulletin board at the library, and I've seen that one old lady, the one who lives in that huge mansion over on the river, at the library. Also, the Bon Appétit . . ."

"What's that?"

"The gourmet grocery store. I went in there the other day to buy saffron. There were chauffeurs there, picking up grocery orders. And there was an old woman at the meat counter, wearing three big strands of pearls and a silk dress, carrying a cane and complaining that her lamb chops weren't thick enough. Lamb chops, incidentally, cost $5.79 a pound at the Bon Appétit."

"That's just the kind of old lady I need," said Anastasia. "I'm going to go up to my room right now and write my résumé."

"What about the dishes?"

Anastasia groaned. "Mom, what's more important? The dishes? Or my entire future?"

"If I wash them, will you come down later and dry them?"

Anastasia bowed dramatically. "Anastasia Krupnik, at your service," she said.

"Anastasia atcherservice," said her father, laughing, imitating Sam with his mouth full of peas.

"Anastasia Atcher Service," said Anastasia. It sounded kind of good. Distinctive. Maybe someday it would be a worldwide corporation.

## ANASTASIA ATCHER SERVICE

**Available:** Companion to elderly, wealthy woman, like in mystery novels by Mary Roberts Rinehart (you can find these at the public library if you have never read one). This Companion is a young woman of good breeding, but her family has fallen on hard times so she needs to earn her living. Her duties are that she is always patient and kind to her employer even if the employer is sometimes grouchy. She pours tea a lot. She reads aloud to her employer, like Gothic novels and stuff, and after each chapter they can discuss romance and give each other advice about love if either one of them has an admirer. The Companion advises her employer about what jewelry to wear, like if three diamond necklaces at one time is tacky, the Companion would tell her so, in a kind and tactful way of course. The Companion pulls down the shades when the employer wants to take a nap in the afternoon, and then she wakes her up if necessary, like if the Vicar comes to call or something. And if the employer is in a wheelchair, the Companion pushes it.

**Résumé:** This part is supposed to be about experience and qualifications. I don't have a lot of experience with wealthy women, but I do with elderly women because once I had a grandmother who lived to be ninety-two. I was always very patient and kind with her, and sometimes we talked about romance, even though at that time I was only ten and hadn't experienced any romance yet. Now I am twelve and have been through some things, so I know more about it. I am good at making and pouring tea if nobody messes around and louses it up. I have never pushed a wheelchair, but I know I would be good at it because I pushed my brother's baby carriage for about one million hours and never once dumped him out. And I come from a family of good breeding, although they have hard times because my father is an English professor and my mother is an artist, so they don't make much money and can't raise my allowance, which is why I desperately need a job.

I could ride to the employer's mansion on my bike, so the chauffeur wouldn't need to pick me up, unless maybe if it was raining really hard.

Anastasia Krupnik                    Salary negotiable
797-8119

# 2

"I'm scared stiff," said Anastasia. "I'm so nervous, I might faint. What is that pill that people take to calm their nerves? Valium? Do you have any Valium?"

"Good heavens," said her mother. "Of course I don't. I've never taken Valium in my life. I never even take aspirin. Why are you so nervous? Just the other day you said you wouldn't be, if you got a job."

"Well, I misjudged. I never in my entire life had a job before, and now I do, and I'm scared stiff. What if she doesn't like me? Old ladies have to *like* their Companions, because they entrust them with their jewels and their personal mail and stuff."

"Anastasia. Of course she'll like you. *Everybody* likes you."

"Do I look all right? I haven't had a dress on in about two years. The last time I wore a dress was to Grandmother's funeral, I think. It's a good thing you bought me some dresses and skirts last spring."

"You didn't think so at the time. I practically had to bribe you to get you to try them on at the store. I *did* have to bribe you, come to think of it. I had to buy you that terrible tee shirt, the one with the fluorescent vampire on it."

"That was a good shirt. Too bad it shrank in the wash. Anyway, thank you for making me get the dresses. Seriously, do I look okay?"

"You look terrific, Anastasia. You really do. You're going to be a very beautiful woman someday."

Anastasia made a face. "I wish I could see without my glasses. Can I get contact lenses when I'm older?"

Her mother groaned. "Anastasia, we need a new refrigerator. The roof needs repairs. Don't talk to me about contact lenses."

"Well, now that I have a job, I can start saving money. Maybe I'll buy you a refrigerator. I'll buy myself some contacts. I'll get Sam an electric train. And I'll buy Dad that stereo he likes at the Radio Shack. And I'll buy . . ."

"Anastasia. Don't go overboard. What is she paying you, anyway?"

"I don't know. She said we would discuss it today. But I'm sure it'll be a lot. She's *very* rich. You should see her house. Did I tell you I rode my bike past her house?"

"Anastasia, you described her house in detail at dinner last night. Nobody else got a chance to say anything at dinner last night. I spent most of yesterday afternoon trying a new recipe. Cannelloni alla romana. It took *hours*. And nobody even got a chance to say they liked it, because you were going on and on about Mrs. Bellingham's house."

"I'm sorry. I liked it. I must have liked it, because I ate it. Did it really take hours to make it?"

"Hours. There were two separate sauces. You didn't even notice. One of them had chicken livers in it, and . . ."

"Mom! Did that have *liver* in it? You know I hate liver! Did you sneak liver into that? And I *ate* it? Why didn't you tell me it was liver? You rat!"

"You never gave me a chance. You talked nonstop the entire meal. Mrs. Bellingham's house. Mrs. Bellingham's cars. Mrs. Bellingham's gardens. Mrs. Bellingham's this, Mrs. Bellingham's that . . ."

"I can't believe you did that to me. Liver. That's treachery. It really is: treachery. Do you think I still have some in my stomach? I might have to throw up."

"You don't have time to throw up. You're going to be late for your first day at work if you don't leave right away."

Anastasia stomped off, muttering. "What are we going to have for dinner tonight?" she called from the front door. *"Brains?"*

"Meat loaf," said her mother. "You're safe."

"If I make enough money, I might start eating in

restaurants," called Anastasia, as she headed to the garage for her bike.

*

Mrs. Ferris Bellingham had called on Saturday, two days before. Anastasia had spent Friday tacking her notices up on bulletin boards around town. At the Bon Appétit gourmet grocery store. In the vestibule of the Unitarian Church. In the library. The country club. The hospital. Everyplace she could think of where rich old ladies might hang out.

Someone who had lost a Siamese cat had had the same idea. Everyplace Anastasia tacked her notice, there was one that offered a reward for a Siamese cat, wearing a red collar, who answered to the name of Sari.

Anastasia thought the cat person really had the wrong idea. A Siamese cat wouldn't be hanging around the library or the country club. A Siamese cat would be in the back alleys, by the trash and garbage, or at the dump. The owner should have hung the notices in those places. Some people don't think things through very carefully.

Anastasia had, though. And on Saturday the telephone had rung.

"Hello?" said Anastasia.

"Willa Bellingham here," said a very loud voice. "Mrs. Ferris Bellingham."

It took a second for Anastasia to figure out how to respond to that. "Anastasia Krupnik here," she said, after a hesitation. "Anastasia Atcher Service."

"You're twelve," said Mrs. Bellingham's loud voice. "That is not very old."

Anastasia shrugged and said the first thing that came into her mind. "It's older than eleven," she pointed out.

"You're seeking employment," said the voice. "You have a rather whimsical way of going about it."

Anastasia didn't know what *whimsical* meant. "Yes, I guess I do," she said. "But it works. At least you called me up."

Mrs. Ferris Bellingham chuckled. "Indeed. Be here Monday at two."

"Be where?" Anastasia asked.

There was a silence. "Are you perhaps new in town?"

"Yes. We moved here last month from Cambridge."

"Bellmeadow Farm. Ask anyone how to find it. I will see you promptly at two. I will discuss the terms of employment with you at that time. Be properly dressed."

"Yes, ma'am," said Anastasia.

Mrs. Ferris Bellingham hung up without saying good-by. She didn't even say she would send her chauffeur if it rained on Monday. Or what she meant by properly dressed.

✿

Anastasia had gone out on her bike to Bellmeadow Farm on Sunday, just for a reconnaissance trip. To look it over. She leaned her bike against the stone wall and stood on tiptoe to peer over it. "Farm" was a fake name, she had decided. There were no cows, no hayfields, no tractors. There were acres of green lawn like a golf course, with sprinklers whirring everywhere; and at the end of a long, curving driveway lined with trees she could see the immense stone house, so large it looked like a school or hospital. Two large black cars like presidential limousines were parked in the driveway.

Anastasia remembered a book she had hated when she was younger. *Rebecca of Sunnybrook Farm.* She made up a new book title. *Anastasia of Bellmeadow Farm.* She liked the sound of it.

Now, riding to her first day on the job, she decided that if Mrs. Ferris Bellingham wanted to adopt her, she would probably say yes. She was still very, very mad at her mother about the liver.

&ast;

Anastasia went directly to the back door. It seemed about three miles around the huge house, and it certainly would have been easier to ring the front doorbell. But she had decided, on her way, that it would be appropriate to go to the back on her first day. Later, after she was fully installed as Companion, of course she would enter by the front. Probably she would have her own key.

Later, too, she would call Mrs. Bellingham by her first name, Willa. But in the beginning she would call her Mrs. Bellingham, she decided. Probably at first Mrs. Bellingham would call her Miss Krupnik. Until they became close friends.

She leaned her bike against a tree and knocked on the

back door. After a moment it was opened by a very fat woman. Anastasia was startled. She hadn't expected Mrs. Bellingham to be fat. She hadn't sounded fat on the phone. Also, Willa sounded like a tall, thin name. But names could be deceiving, Anastasia knew. Sam Krupnik, for example, sounded like a tall, bearded man. In reality, Sam Krupnik was a two-and-a-half-year-old brat who still wore Pampers at night. Eventually he would grow into his tall, bearded name; in the meantime, he was a pain in the neck.

"Hello, Mrs. Bellingham," she said politely. "I'm Anas——"

The woman interrupted her. "I'm Edna Fox," she said. "I'm the housekeeper. And you're the girl Mrs. B's taken on. Good thing. We're up to our ears. Come on in."

Mrs. Fox led her into a kitchen that seemed as large as the entire downstairs of the Krupniks' house.

Two women wearing aprons were standing near a large double sink, peeling carrots and potatoes. They looked over and smiled at Anastasia. Anastasia smiled back. It was important for the Companion to stay on good terms with the kitchen help, she knew from the novels she had read.

"Rachel and Gloria," said Mrs. Fox, indicating the two aproned women.

"How do you do," said Anastasia politely.

"Hi, there," said Rachel and Gloria.

"Here's an apron for you," said the housekeeper, handing a flowered apron to Anastasia. "Let's get you started.

We are out straight. Two of the help quit last week, without any notice at all. And there's a party tomorrow. You can start on the silverware. The polish is over there."

Anastasia unfolded the apron, puzzled. A Companion wasn't supposed to wear an apron. Especially an apron like this. It was the kind that went on over your head, the kind old ladies wore. Also, it was much too big.

She put it on, tied it behind her back, and stood there, embarrassed. Heaped on a wooden kitchen table that looked roughly the size of a football field was a mound of silverware larger than any mound of silverware Anastasia had ever seen.

"I wonder if there's some mistake," she said timidly to Mrs. Fox. "I thought I was supposed to . . ."

"Mistake isn't the word for it," said Mrs. Fox. "Disaster is what it is. To invite ten people for lunch, with two of the help gone. Madness. Catastrophe. Here are some rags."

Mrs. Fox thrust a handful of cloths into Anastasia's hand and disappeared through a door.

Of course. Anastasia sorted it out in her mind, and she understood. It was an emergency situation. Even the Companion had to pitch in and help in an emergency.

Well, okay. She was a good sport. Companions always were. Anastasia picked up the first of twelve million spoons and began to polish.

She polished.

And polished.

And polished.

"I don't mind doing this kind of thing in an emergency," she said cheerfully to Rachel and Gloria, who continued their peeling silently.

One rag after another turned black as Anastasia polished. After what seemed hours (but it wasn't; she looked at her watch, and only half an hour had passed), there was a large pile of polished spoons and forks beside her on the table. There was a still larger pile of unpolished ones still in the center. But she made a bundle of the finished ones in her apron and took them over to the sink to wash off the polish.

"Excuse me," she said to Rachel and Gloria, "I'm just going to rinse these off." And she dumped them into the sink.

There was a sudden, deafening crunch.

"Omigod," said Rachel. Or maybe it was Gloria. One of them pushed Anastasia aside and flipped a switch. The crunching noise stopped. The kitchen was very, very silent.

"The garbage disposal was running," said Rachel.

"For the peelings," said Gloria.

"Oh," said Anastasia.

One of them reached into the drain and pulled out a silver spoon. Or what had once been a silver spoon. Now it looked like a piece of abstract sculpture that Anastasia had once seen at the Institute of Contemporary Art.

"I didn't know the disposal was on," she said miserably.

"Obviously," said Mrs. Fox, who suddenly appeared

behind her and took the mashed spoon out of her hand.

"It has a kind of interesting shape now," said Anastasia.

Rachel and Gloria turned away and began peeling again. Mrs. Fox didn't say anything.

"Good thing there are a billion more spoons," said Anastasia.

Mrs. Fox left the kitchen again.

Anastasia slowly rinsed and dried the rest of the polished silverware. She arranged it on the table, picked up a clean rag, and began polishing again.

"This is a good way to get in practice," she said after a while, "because I suppose I'll be polishing Mrs. Bellingham's jewelry when I start my regular job."

Rachel and Gloria looked at her curiously and went on peeling carrots and potatoes.

"Of course I won't drop her diamonds down the disposal," said Anastasia. She meant it as a joke. But neither Rachel nor Gloria laughed.

It sure was *boring*, working in a kitchen with people who had no sense of humor. Much as Anastasia hated doing dishes at home, still she and her mother always laughed a lot. If Sam came in the kitchen while they were washing dishes, they put soapsuds on his chin and made him a beard. Sam liked that.

Anastasia began to feel homesick for Sam.

She remembered a silly thing her mother sometimes did. Sometimes her mother picked up a plate, looked into it, and said, "I can *see* myself in this china!" — imitating a TV commercial.

Anastasia picked up a small silver tray she had just polished, looked into it, and said dramatically, "I can *see* myself in this china!"

Rachel and Gloria glanced over at her as if she were crazy. Neither of them laughed.

Anastasia put the tray down and sighed. She *had* seen herself in the tray. She had silver polish on her nose. Her hair was a mess. She looked like a household drudge.

She felt very, very homesick.

She picked up the millionth fork and polished.

And polished.

✿

At four o'clock Mrs. Fox came back into the kitchen. Rachel and Gloria had finished their peeling. They were working silently at something in another corner of the kitchen. The pile of silverware was almost finished.

Mrs. Fox nodded to Anastasia. "Mrs. B wants to see you now," she said.

At last. Anastasia didn't mind being a good sport in an emergency, but two solid hours of silver-polishing was enough. She was ready to get on with her real job.

She took off her apron, wiped the silver polish from her nose with a damp cloth, and smoothed her hair.

She followed Mrs. Fox out of the kitchen. Down a hall. Through a door. Down another hall lined with paintings. Through an oak-paneled room with wall-to-wall bookcases. Across another hall. Into a sunny room filled with plants, where a gray-haired woman sat in a wicker chair, working on a piece of needlepoint.

Mrs. Bellingham. At last. And she was exactly as Anastasia had pictured her. Everything was going to be okay. Starting now, she could forget the drudgery of the emergency silver-polishing, and she and Mrs. Bellingham could get on with the business of Companionship. If she were older, Mrs. Bellingham would offer her a glass of sherry now. Probably she wouldn't offer sherry to someone who was twelve. But that was okay. Anastasia didn't like sherry anyway. She'd settle for some iced tea. Mrs. Fox had disappeared. Probably Mrs. Fox was getting the tea.

Mrs. Bellingham lit a cigarette. Anastasia hoped she wouldn't offer her one. To be polite she would have to take it, but she really hated cigarettes.

But Mrs. Bellingham snapped the silver cigarette case closed and inhaled her cigarette without offering one to Anastasia.

"Well," said Mrs. Bellingham, "we didn't give you much time to break in, did we? Put you right to work!"

Anastasia smiled. "I understand about emergencies, Mrs. Bellingham. Everybody has to pitch in. And I enjoyed getting to know the kitchen staff. That's important, I think." It was sort of a lie — she hadn't enjoyed Rachel and Gloria at all — but it seemed the right thing to say.

"Indeed. Did Mrs. Fox tell you about the luncheon tomorrow?"

"She told me that there was a party tomorrow."

"A family lunch. My granddaughter's birthday."

Anastasia smiled. That was wonderful, she thought. She could just write off the silver-polishing afternoon as a bad beginning. Tomorrow she would get to know the family. She would begin her Companion duties for real. Tonight she would have to think seriously about Conversation Topics. Not politics or religion, she knew. Literature, probably. Tonight she would review in her mind all the books she had ever read. *Gone With the Wind* was one of her favorites. She could talk to people at the luncheon about *Gone With the Wind*. Why Scarlett didn't marry Ashley Wilkes. Stuff like that.

What a terrific job I have, thought Anastasia happily.

"I would like you here promptly at eleven A.M.," said Mrs. Bellingham.

Suddenly Anastasia thought of a problem. She had nothing to wear to a luncheon. She was already wearing her only decent dress, and it had smears of silver polish on it. What she needed was a Basic Black dress. Never in a million years would her mother take her out tonight to buy a Basic Black dress.

She couldn't borrow a dress from Mrs. Bellingham. They weren't the same size. And their taste seemed to be a little different.

"Do you have a dark skirt?" Mrs. Bellingham asked. She had read Anastasia's mind. What a terrific relationship they were going to have, Anastasia thought.

"Yes," she said. "A dark blue denim wraparound."

"Well, that will do, I guess. Wear it with a tailored white blouse. Those sandals you're wearing will be all right."

A denim skirt and a white blouse didn't seem too terrific for an elegant luncheon. Maybe Mrs. Bellingham planned to lend her some jewelry, thought Anastasia.

"Mrs. Fox will give you a white apron," said Mrs. Bellingham.

A *white apron?* Anastasia had been thinking along the lines of a diamond necklace. Suddenly she had a strange feeling that things weren't exactly what she thought they were.

Mrs. Bellingham inhaled her cigarette again. "The luncheon will be buffet," she said, "so you won't have to serve at the table. But be sure to empty ashtrays, keep water glasses filled, that sort of thing."

Anastasia's vision of herself discussing Scarlett O'Hara with the guests at lunch faded and blurred.

I'm the *maid*, she thought in despair, realizing the truth in a horrible sudden flash.

Mrs. Bellingham was making some notes on a pad of paper. Anastasia stood there watching, stricken with disappointment. In her mind she began to compose a letter. She would write it tonight and deliver it in the morning. "Dear Mrs. Bellingham," it would say, "I have decided to go into another profession."

"Now," said Mrs. Bellingham, looking up, "do you have any questions?"

Yes, thought Anastasia angrily. What right did you have to answer an ad for a Companion, for Pete's sake, and then turn someone into a scullery maid, without even *asking* her? Who the heck do you think you *are?*

She almost said those things aloud. "Yes," she began, in a firm voice. "What —"

"Oh, of course," Mrs. Bellingham interrupted her.

"Your wages. You will be paid two-fifty an hour, and since you arrived at two this afternoon . . ."

Wait a *minute*, thought Anastasia, getting madder by the second. Two-fifty an hour? That's baby-sitting pay, for Pete's sake! I was thinking in terms of ten dollars an hour. I might be willing to settle for seven-fifty, but . . .

Mrs. Bellingham was going on and on. ". . . so today you have earned five dollars. However . . ."

And after the "however," she reached under her needlepoint and held up the mashed silver spoon. Anastasia's heart sank. Five hundred billion silver spoons in that kitchen, and Mrs. Bellingham was — she could hear it coming — going to charge her for that one spoon? Probably it cost at least five dollars, too. Her whole crummy afternoon's pay!

"The price of this at Shreve's is thirty-five dollars," Mrs. Bellingham was going on.

THIRTY-FIVE DOLLARS? Anastasia couldn't believe it. It was too horrible to be happening to her. It was a nightmare.

"So that debacle will cost you twelve more hours of work," Mrs. Bellingham said firmly. It was what she had been calculating on her notepad.

A what? thought Anastasia. A *bockle?* She didn't even know what a bockle was. It looked like an ordinary silver spoon to her. Just her luck to put a bockle down the garbage disposal.

She stood there numbly and said nothing. Surely Mrs. Bellingham was finished with her now. She couldn't possibly think of any more humiliations.

Wrong. She could, and did. One more.

"You're going into the seventh grade, I suppose?" Mrs. Bellingham asked.

Anastasia nodded.

"So is my granddaughter, Daphne," said Mrs. Bellingham pleasantly. "Tomorrow is her thirteenth birthday. So you'll have an opportunity to meet one of your classmates."

It was worse than the thirty-five-dollar silver bockle. Much worse. It was the ultimate humiliation. She was going to meet one of her classmates — someone who might have been her *friend*, for Pete's sake, in a town where she knew practically no one — and she would be wearing an apron and refilling the water glasses.

Anastasia cried as she rode her bike home. It was starting to rain, and the light drizzle mixed with the tears rolling down her cheeks.

Once, she thought bitterly — only a few hours ago — I thought that if it rained, the chauffeur would drive me home in a limousine.

Her mother was in the kitchen when Anastasia came through the back door.

"Meat loaf in an hour!" called her mother cheerfully. "How did your first day at work go?"

Anastasia headed up the back stairs toward her room on the third floor.

"Just fine!" she called down the stairs in a fake happy voice.

In a million years — in a million *billion* years — she would never let anyone know.

# 3

Exactly one hour and twenty-seven minutes after she had vowed never to let anyone in the entire world know, ever, what a disaster her day had been, Anastasia burst into tears at the dinner table.

Anastasia had not burst into tears at the dinner table for six and a half years. She could remember the last time, even though it was so long ago. She had had a big fight with her very best friend, Jenny MacCauley, that afternoon. Just before dinner, Jenny had called her on the phone and said, "You are no longer invited to my birthday party Saturday, nyah nyah."

Anastasia had said, "Nyah nyah to you, too," and hung up. But she had burst into tears at the dinner table. She was in first grade then.

But now she was almost thirteen. It was incredibly embarrassing to start to cry in public when you were almost thirteen. Even if the public was just your family.

"Excuse me," said Sam very quickly, with a wide-eyed look, when Anastasia began to cry. "I have to go to the bathroom, I think." And he climbed out of his highchair and left the dining room, still wearing his bib.

Even through her sobs, Anastasia knew Sam was lying. Normally it took bribes and threats to get Sam to go to the bathroom. As bright as he was, Sam still liked to wear diapers. It was the one thing he was still babyish and dumb about. That, and his ragged security blanket.

Her parents both stopped eating and stared at her in dismay.

"Sweetheart, what's *wrong?*" asked her mother.

Anastasia couldn't talk. She just kept crying.

Her father left his chair, came around to Anastasia's side of the table, and put his arms around her. He rocked her back and forth.

Through her tears, Anastasia could see Sam peeking at her from the dining room door. He had wrapped his security blanket around his hand and had his thumb in his mouth.

"Make Sam stop staring at me," she said, weeping.

"Sam Krupnik," said her mother sternly, "either come in here and sit down, or go away. Don't peek around the door like that."

Sam scampered away.

Finally Anastasia's sobs turned to gulps and deep breaths.

"She made me wear an apron," she wailed, "not a cute apron like Dad wears when he grills steaks, but a flowered apron like a cleaning lady wears, and I was just like a maid, I had to stay in the kitchen with the maids, and I wasn't a Companion at all, I had to clean five billion pieces of silverware, and I didn't mean to but I dropped a bockle down the disposal, I thought it was just a spoon, but it wasn't, and she said it cost thirty-five dollars at Shreve's, and now I owe her thirty-five dollars, so I have to be a maid *forever*, and tomorrow I have to be a maid when her granddaughter is there, and her granddaughter is thirteen, she might have been my *friend*, for Pete's sake, and she didn't offer me a glass of sherry or anything —"

"Whoa," said her father. "I'm confused. The granddaughter is thirteen and was supposed to offer you a glass of sherry?"

"No! You're not listening!"

"Well, can you talk a little more slowly?"

Anastasia took a very deep breath. Her crying spell seemed to have ended. Thank goodness. Anastasia hated to cry. It made her look as if she had Troubled Skin, for Pete's sake, and she *didn't*. She had stringy hair and skinny legs, but she did not have, and never *had* had, Troubled Skin.

She wiped her eyes and told the whole story, very slowly.

"Holy Moley," said her father.

"*Dad,*" said Anastasia angrily. She hated it when her father said Holy Moley. It was left over from his childhood, or some weird thing.

"Sorry," said her father apologetically. "It was what Billy Batson, the young reporter, used to say in comic books. When things were absolutely awful, he would say, 'Holy Moley!' Then he yelled, 'CAPTAIN MARVEL!' and he turned into Captain Marvel and could solve everything with his super powers."

"Myron," said Mrs. Krupnik meaningfully. She had noticed Anastasia becoming more and more impatient.

"No," Myron Krupnik went on, "maybe it wasn't Billy Batson who said Holy Moley. Maybe, come to think of it, it was Freddy Freeman, the crippled newsboy. He was in the same comic books."

"*Dad!* Quit it!" Anastasia was almost beginning to cry again.

"Well, it's just that I wish I could turn into Captain Marvel. It would be easier to solve your problem if I were Captain Marvel."

"Daddy," said Sam, who had crept quietly back into the dining room, "*I* think you're Captain Marvel."

His father lifted Sam onto his lap. "You know, Anastasia," he said, "that woman — what's her name again?"

"Mrs. Bellingham."

"Mrs. Bellingham. Right. You know, she really took advantage of you. You had described clearly on your advertisement exactly what kind of job you were looking for."

"Right. Companion."

"And she put you to work at something different, without asking your permission."

"She put me right to work as a *maid*."

"Yes, I think it's fair to say that. And under other circumstances you certainly would be justified in quitting."

"What other circumstances?" asked Anastasia. "The circumstances are that she made me be a *maid*."

"That's true. Unfortunately, you mashed something in the garbage disposal. I didn't exactly understand what you said it was."

"A bockle."

"Well, I don't know what that is. But let's assume that she was correct, that it was worth thirty-five dollars."

"Why do we have to assume that? Maybe she was lying. Mom, would you call Shreve's? Ask Shreve's if a bockle really costs thirty-five dollars?"

Her mother looked at her watch. "It's six-thirty. Shreve's is closed. Anyway, Anastasia, you said it was silver, didn't you?"

"Yes. It was definitely silver. I know because I polished it. It looked like a spoon."

"Well, if it was silver and came from Shreve's, it was thirty-five dollars. Frankly, Anastasia, you're lucky it wasn't a hundred and thirty-five dollars."

Anastasia groaned.

"So," said her father, "you do owe Mrs. Bellingham thirty-five dollars."

"Only thirty," Anastasia pointed out angrily. "I worked five dollars' worth today."

"Thirty, then. I don't suppose you have thirty dollars to pay her back, do you?"

"Dad," said Anastasia wearily, "the reason I was looking for a job was because I am broke."

Her father lifted Sam down from his lap. "Sam," he said, "climb up in your highchair and finish your dinner, will you?"

Sam trotted around to his highchair, climbed in, and ate a bite of meat loaf. "I have four pennies," he said. "You can have my four pennies, Anastasia."

"That's okay, Sam," said Anastasia. "Thanks, anyway."

"Anastasia," said her father, "I feel sorry enough for you that if I had thirty extra dollars I would pay for the blasted bockle myself. But frankly, moving out here cost so much, what with having to buy a car and a lawn mower and everything, that I'm flat broke, too. Katherine, I don't suppose you . . ."

"No," said Mrs. Krupnik sadly. "I won't get paid for these photography illustrations until I finish them. And I'm barely halfway through. I'm really sorry, Anastasia."

"Oh, Mom. Dad. That's okay. I was the one who mashed the bockle. I guess I'm just going to have to keep working for old Bellingham."

"Bellybutton." Sam giggled. "Old dumb Mrs. Bellybutton."

Anastasia laughed. It was the first time she had laughed all day.

"I'll just have to figure out a way to survive it. Being a *maid*, for Pete's sake. And tomorrow her granddaughter's going to be there. How humiliating. Has anything that humiliating ever happened to you guys?"

Her parents thought.

"Yes," her mother said finally. "A couple of years ago a publisher in New York called and asked if I was interested in illustrating a book about Houston rockets. They were paying a lot of money. I said sure, I thought I could do that very well. So they asked me to work up some sample drawings and bring them down to show to the author.

"I was lying when I said I could do that very well. I didn't know anything at all about rockets. But I got a lot of books about rockets and missiles and the space industry. And I spent about a week making rough sketches of jets and guided missiles and engines and launching pads and satellites and various kinds of rockets. Then I put them all in my portfolio and went off to New York. I really thought they were pretty good."

"What happened? Weren't they any good? Did the people laugh when they saw them?"

"Well, we all met in a fancy room at the publishing company. A couple of editors and the art director and the author. They were all sitting around a mahogany table. I was wearing my tweed suit, I remember. I don't think I've worn that since," her mother said.

"What *happened?*"

"I opened my portfolio and took out all those sketches and spread them out on the table. I was really pretty proud of them. But there was a terrible silence."

"Why? Why was there a terrible silence?"

"And then one person started to laugh. Then another. In a minute they were all laughing. They couldn't stop laughing. The fat one — the art director, I think it was — had tears rolling down his cheeks. Someone had to bring him a glass of water, because they were afraid he was going to have a heart attack from laughing."

"Why were they laughing? You're a good artist, Mom!" Anastasia felt terribly sorry for her mother, being humiliated that way.

Her mother began to laugh. "Because they were doing a book about a basketball team! The Houston Rockets is a basketball team!"

"I knew that," said Sam. "I see them on TV."

"Oh, Mom!" said Anastasia. "The rats! That wasn't fair! They should have told you! They shouldn't have laughed!"

"Well," said her mother, "it was humiliating. But I survived it. They found someone else to do the basketball book. And they gave me a job doing a book about the astronauts."

"How about you, Dad? Have you ever been humiliated?" Somehow it was making Anastasia feel better, knowing that other people had been humiliated.

Her father blushed. You could always tell when he was blushing, because he was bald. When he blushed, the top of his head turned red.

"Of course I have," he said with dignity. "No one lives to be forty-seven years old without being humiliated a few times."

"What happened?"

He was still blushing. "I don't want to talk about it," he said.

"That's not fair. Mom told about hers. And I told you about what happened to me today."

He groaned. "Promise you won't ever tell anyone."

"I promise."

Her father looked around the dining room to make sure there were no spies listening. He looked down at his plate for a minute, embarrassed. Then he looked up.

"Last semester I gave an hour-long lecture on Social Comedy in Eighteenth-Century England. The students — there were eighty-seven students in the lecture hall — kept laughing."

"But that was okay. You were lecturing about comedy," said Anastasia.

"That wasn't why they were laughing." Her father began playing with his fork.

"Why were they?"

He leaned his elbows on the table and put his face into his hands. The top of his head was bright pink.

"My fly was unzipped," he said after a while. "The whole hour. I didn't realize it until afterward."

"Dad! That's terrible! Someone should have *told* you! That wasn't fair, for them to laugh!"

But next thing she knew, Anastasia was laughing herself. So was her father. And her mother. Sam wasn't; he was busy trying to make an airplane out of a piece of lettuce.

"Well," said her father, still chuckling. "I survived, just as your mother did."

"I guess I will too, then," said Anastasia. "I'll survive being a maid."

"What are you going to say to Mrs. Bellingham when you go to work tomorrow?"

Anastasia thought. "I'll smile," she said, "and I'll say, 'Anastasia Atcher Service.' "

✤

But much later, as she was going to bed, she thought of something else. Not that she would say. But that she would *do*.

# 4

The worst part of the problem, Anastasia had realized, thinking about it the night before, was not the humiliation of being a maid. She could survive that, the way her mother and her father had survived their humiliations and had even been able to laugh about them afterward. Someday Anastasia would be able to tell her own children about the summer she was a maid, and she would be able to laugh about it.

What she might not survive was being a maid in front of Daphne Bellingham, who would be her classmate in seventh grade this fall. *That* was the problem she would have to solve.

And she had decided to solve it by going to work in

disguise. She would disguise herself as a middle-aged woman.

❀

By ten in the morning, no one was at home except Anastasia. Her father was off teaching his summer school class, and her mother had taken Sam to visit the nursery school he would be going to in the fall.

Dumb old Sam didn't understand about nursery schools. He thought that he was going to learn to read. He had insisted on going off with Volume One of the *Encyclopaedia Britannica* in his stroller with him. He wanted to learn to read the part about airplanes.

Well, thought Anastasia with some satisfaction, maybe today Sam will be humiliated. Maybe the nursery school people would laugh.

Anastasia went into her parents' bedroom and opened one of her mother's bureau drawers. She felt a little guilty, because she wasn't ordinarily a sneaky sort of person.

But this was a very necessary part of her disguise.

She took out one of her mother's bras. Then she went into the bathroom and put it on. Carefully she stuffed each side of it with Kleenex. Then she put on the white blouse that Mrs. Bellingham had told her to wear.

But when she looked at herself in the mirror from different angles, she realized the Kleenex didn't work. It looked lumpy and gross.

So she took the Kleenex out and threw it away.

She thought for a minute and went back to her

mother's bureau. This time she snitched two pairs of pantyhose.

Back in the bathroom, she put a pair of pantyhose into each side of the bra. They were rounder, softer, more natural-looking than the Kleenex.

But when she looked at herself sideways in the mirror, she groaned.

It looked like Dolly Parton.

Also, it made her feel funny. She couldn't even see her feet, because she had to look over the mountain of pantyhose. So she took them out and thought some more.

After a few minutes, feeling even more guilty, because now she was going to owe her mother at least $1.49, she found a pair of scissors and cut one pair of pantyhose in half. She stuffed one rolled-up half into each side of the bra.

Now she looked into the mirror and smiled. It was perfect. She walked around the bathroom a bit to make sure the pantyhose didn't come loose or shift around, but they seemed quite secure. Maybe because her blouse buttoned so tightly over them.

Next, she opened the bathroom drawer where her mother kept make-up.

She took out the mascara and took off her glasses in order to color her eyelashes.

But she couldn't see without her glasses. Her face in the mirror was blurred.

She put her glasses back on. Now she could see her eyelashes, but she couldn't reach them with the mascara.

"Rats," said Anastasia to herself, and she sat down on

the rim of the bathtub to think. How on earth did Helen Keller put on mascara?

Braille.

Anastasia took off her glasses, and put mascara on her eyelashes without looking. Then she put her glasses back on. It didn't look too bad.

She darkened her eyebrows with an eyebrow pencil, reaching around the rims of her glasses. When she leaned forward toward the mirror, her pantyhose bosom bumped into the bathroom sink and squashed; but Anastasia noticed that it puffed right out again when she stood back. Much better than Kleenex.

Finally, very carefully, she sprinkled Johnson's Baby Powder on her hair and smoothed it in with her hands. Then, with a rubber band and a handful of bobby pins, she twisted her hair into a bun and pinned it at the back of her head. Her light hair looked gray from the powder.

She dabbed a little pink lipstick on her lips, straightened her blouse and skirt, and went to stand in front of the full-length mirror that was on the back of her parents' bedroom door.

With grayish hair, dark eyebrows, pink lipstick, and the pantyhose bosom, she figured she looked about forty years old. From her mother's closet, she borrowed a large black leather pocketbook and hung it over her shoulder. Now she definitely looked forty years old. She could be elected President of the League of Women Voters without any trouble at all.

It was twenty of eleven. Anastasia Krupnik, age forty,

with the black pocketbook thumping against her hip, got on her bike and rode to Bellmeadow Farm.

✣

"Good," said Edna Fox at the back door, "you're right on time. There's lots to do. You can hang your purse in that closet there. You don't have a lot of money in it, do you? I'm not going to take the responsibility if . . ."

"No," said Anastasia, and rolled her eyes. Good grief. In debt for thirty dollars, working as a maid in order to pay back thirty whole dollars, and someone asks if you have a lot of money in your purse. If she had a lot of money, for Pete's sake, she'd pay it to Mrs. Bellingham for her crummy bockle, get on her bike, and be gone so fast they'd never know what had happened.

Too bad she had to put her pocketbook in the closet. It was part of her middle-age disguise. Still, maids didn't usually carry their pocketbooks around while they served lunch, Anastasia realized.

Edna Fox handed her an apron.

Good grief, thought Anastasia. Yesterday's apron had covered her whole body. She didn't want to hide her pantyhose bosom. It would ruin the whole effect.

But the apron was a tiny white one, one that tied around the waist and had no top to it. Good. She tied it carefully, with her back to Mrs. Fox, and to Rachel and Gloria, who were at the sink. She had to hold the bosom up with one hand while she arranged the waistband of the apron. The bra was a little loose. The bosom was a little lower than she would have liked. Still, maybe that would make her look even older. Anastasia had noticed that old ladies' bosoms began to be pretty low sometimes. Maybe she looked fifty instead of forty. Fifty was even better.

"You look different," said Mrs. Fox. "Are you okay?"

"I'm just wearing my hair differently today," said Anastasia. "I'm fine." But she realized that Mrs. Fox was looking at the bosom, not the hair.

Well, tough. It was not, Anastasia thought, unheard of for a girl to grow quite quickly in that respect. Once, years ago, she had had a baby-sitter named Marcia, who practically *overnight,* for Pete's sake, had changed from flat-chested to —

But Mrs. Fox interrupted her thoughts.

"The company's all here," she said. "They're on the terrace, having cocktails. You can start taking trays of food to the dining room table."

Anastasia carried a large silver platter of sliced turkey and ham into the dining room. Wide glass doors were opened onto the flagstone terrace, and she could see the people sitting there. She could see Mrs. Bellingham, her arch enemy, sitting in a wrought-iron chair that resembled a throne. Typical, thought Anastasia.

She moved quietly to the side of the glass doors and stood where she was hidden by the folds of an opened drape. Peeking out, she found Daphne Bellingham, who was sitting on the stone steps, sipping a Coke and looking very bored.

Anastasia had been secretly hoping that Daphne Bellingham would be very ugly, with crooked teeth and Troubled Skin. But she wasn't. She had short, curly blond hair, and tiny gold earrings in pierced ears. She wasn't beautiful. But she was kind of cute.

Rats. Anastasia's parents wouldn't let her have her ears pierced. Not till she was thirteen, they said. She had tried to do it herself once, anyway, with a needle, but her hands kept getting sweaty and the needle slid around too much.

Daphne Bellingham was wearing a yellow-and-white-striped jersey dress, and there was a funny little mark on it. Anastasia squinted at the mark. Of course. The dress had had an alligator on it once, and Daphne Bellingham had pulled the alligator off.

Oh, *rats*. Daphne Bellingham was someone Anastasia would *like*.

Anastasia kicked the carpeting angrily and went back to the kitchen for another tray of food.

"Here," said Edna Fox, and put a large platter into Anastasia's hands. "Hors d'oeuvres. Pass these around, will you? Don't forget to serve the women first."

"I know about stuff like that, Mrs. Fox," said Anastasia with an icy smile.

The platter was filled with some of Anastasia's very favorite things. Deviled eggs. Artichoke leaves with little shrimp on them. Chicken wings. And Anastasia was starving. Her stomach rumbled. She hadn't eaten any breakfast at all because she'd been too busy planning her disguise.

Going through the dining room to the terrace doors,

she decided that she might faint if she didn't eat something. Not a chicken wing, because she would be left with the bone. Not an artichoke-and-shrimp, because she'd be left with the artichoke part that you didn't eat.

She set the platter on the table for a minute, stuffed a deviled egg into her mouth, rearranged the other things to cover the empty space, and headed for the terrace.

She held her mouth very carefully so that no one would notice there was half an egg inside it.

"There you are, dear!" said Mrs. Bellingham in a loud voice. "I want to introduce you to everyone! This is Anastasia . . . What was your last name again?"

Anastasia swallowed the egg whole, and said, "Krupnik," in a strangling voice. Then she hiccuped.

"Excuse me," she said, miserably.

She could hear Daphne Bellingham giggle. Quickly she began passing the platter to the guests. She could hear Mrs. Bellingham rattling off everyone's names. My sister, Mrs. Aldrich Forbes. My daughter-in-law, Caroline Bellingham. My son, John Bellingham. Blah blah blah. Anastasia wasn't even listening. She was trying desperately to keep from hiccuping again. The deviled egg was lodged in her throat somewhere.

"I especially want you to meet the birthday girl. This is my granddaughter, Daphne. Daphne, Anastasia is —"

Anastasia knew exactly what she was going to say. Anastasia is going into the seventh grade. Couldn't Mrs. Bellingham *see* that it was all a mistake, that she was actually middle-aged?

She hurriedly interrupted Daphne's grandmother and said, in her forty-year-old voice, around the remains of the deviled egg and a whole batch of potential hiccups, "I'm glad to meet you, Miss Bellingham. Would you like some hors d'oeuvres?"

She leaned over to offer the platter to Daphne Bellingham. She could hear Daphne stifle a giggle. In a hideous, horrible instant of perception she knew what was happening, and it was too late to do anything about it.

Her whole pantyhose bosom — both sides — was leaning into the platter. It was resting right on the hors d'oeuvres. There were deviled eggs stuck to the bottom side of it.

The other people were talking. They hadn't noticed. But Daphne had. Daphne was almost choking on her Coke. Her shoulders were shaking.

"Whoops!" said Daphne suddenly. "I spilled some Coke on my dress. Anastasia, would you come help me wash it off?"

Mrs. Bellingham tsked-tsked. "Daphne, when will you outgrow that clumsiness? Give her a hand, Anastasia. There's cleaning fluid in the powder room if you need it."

Anastasia put the platter of hors d'oeuvres down in the dining room. The tops of the eggs were a little mashed, but not too badly. You couldn't tell they'd been mashed by a bosom. She followed Daphne through the house to a powder room off the huge front hall. If she walked stiffly, you couldn't see the egg yolk on her front; it was all kind of on the underneath side.

How on earth did Dolly Parton pass a plate of deviled eggs, she wondered grouchily.

"Now then, Miss Bellingham," said Anastasia briskly, in her middle-aged maid's voice, when the two girls were inside the pretty blue-and-green powder room, "let me take care of that stain for you."

Daphne Bellingham hooted with laughter. "Knock it off, Anastasia, whoever you are!" she said. "I didn't spill any Coke. I was just trying to rescue you. What on *earth* do you have stuffed inside your blouse: Kleenex? I did it once with Kleenex when I was trying to get some boy on the high school football team to notice me. But it didn't work. It looked really gross. All my friends laughed, and I ended up pulling it all out in the school library, back behind the reference shelves. I wadded it all up and left it hidden behind a volume of *World's Great Scientists*. What *is* that you have in there?"

"Pantyhose," Anastasia confessed. "I was trying to look forty years old because I didn't want you to know I was going to be in seventh grade. Because your grandmother forced me to be a maid, and it was so embarrassing. Actually, it's even more embarrassing to end up with egg yolk all over my blouse."

Daphne giggled. "Here, I can get the egg off. It's not as bad as you think. Take your blouse off a minute and I'll wash that part. Why on earth did my grandmother make you be a maid? She's such a creep."

Anastasia gave her the blouse, stood there in her mother's bra, and told Daphne the whole story. The night before, it had made her cry. Now, it made her laugh.

"I still owe her thirty dollars," she explained, at the end of the story. "I'll have to be her maid forever." For some reason, the thought of being a maid forever seemed very funny now. Daphne was laughing as she washed the egg smears off the blouse. Anastasia couldn't stop laughing. She was still hiccuping from the deviled egg she had swallowed whole; now she was choking with laughter as well, and tears were running down her face.

"I could take the bosom off" — she giggled — "but what would I do with it? I'd have to carry it back in there. What if your grandmother saw me walking through the dining room with a bra full of pantyhose in my hand?"

"Maybe she'd think it was a new hors d'oeuvre Mrs. Fox had dreamed up," Daphne suggested. "She's so dumb. Hey — you could just stuff it in one of the drawers here, and leave it. Like my Kleenex I left in the library. You and I could be the only two people in town who hide fake bosoms everywhere!"

"No," Anastasia decided, even though she liked the idea of being Bosom Phantoms, "I can't, because it's my mother's bra. I have to sneak it back into her bureau. I guess I'll just leave it on for now." She took the damp blouse from Daphne and put it on.

"Anastasia, your face!"

"What's wrong with my face?" Anastasia looked in the

mirror and groaned. The tears from laughing had made the mascara run down her cheeks, and she was smudged with black.

"Here," said Daphne. "Take off your glasses and I'll wash your face. For heaven's sake, Anastasia, you need a nursemaid. Good thing I was here."

"If you hadn't been here," Anastasia pointed out, "none of this would have happened, because I wouldn't have worn a disguise."

She dried her face and put her glasses back on. "There. Now back to being a maid again."

"You want a cigarette before we go back?" asked Daphne. "I know where my grandmother keeps them."

"No," said Anastasia, startled. "I hate cigarettes."

"Me too." Now Daphne giggled. "But I smoke them because it drives my parents up a wall. I'm practically a juvenile delinquent."

"That's weird," said Anastasia. "I drive my parents up a wall all the time, but I do it accidentally. Why would you do it on purpose?"

"Because of who my parents are, I guess."

Anastasia had forgotten for a moment who Daphne was. Of course. She was Daphne Bellingham. "It must be really weird to be rich," she said. "My parents can't even afford a new refrigerator."

"We're not *rich*," said Daphne.

"Liar. How many rooms in this house — twenty-five? How many servants? How many Cadillacs?"

"This is my grandmother's house," Daphne pointed

out patiently. "My grandmother's rich. Super-rich. But don't you know who my father is?"

"John Bellingham," said Anastasia. "Your grandmother introduced me. I was choking on an egg at the time, in case you didn't notice."

"The *Reverend* John Bellingham," said Daphne, in an ostentatiously solemn voice. "Rector of the Congregational Church. Ministers are never rich. They're poor. They're also *good*. They never do anything bad. It is so incredibly boring, being a minister's kid."

Anastasia thought about that for a minute. "My father doesn't do bad stuff either," she said. "But he's not boring."

"Doesn't he ever swear?"

"Well, he's not foul-mouthed or anything. But *occasionally* he swears. Like when I melted his Billie Holiday records."

"See what I mean? If I melted my father's Billie Holiday records, he wouldn't swear. He'd forgive me or something."

"Oh," said Anastasia. "My father has never forgiven me for that."

"Does your father smoke?"

"A pipe," said Anastasia.

"See? My father doesn't smoke anything, ever. He's too good. Does your father ever get mad?"

"Sure. So does my mom. They yell and stuff."

"My parents don't. Not ever. They're nice, absolutely all the time. Can you imagine how *boring* that is?"

Anastasia wasn't certain. Actually, it sounded sort of pleasant. But she nodded her head.

"So," said Daphne, as if it were all quite logical, "I specialize in being practically a juvenile delinquent."

"Oh," said Anastasia. "Is it fun?"

Daphne shrugged. "When I have a special project, it is," she said. "And now I do. Revenge on my grandmother."

That made Anastasia nervous. "Don't do anything to your grandmother because of *me*, Daphne. I did mash the silver thing, after all. I do owe her the money."

"But she's making you be a *maid*, for heaven's sake. Don't you hate her for that?"

"Well, yes, I guess I do."

"So. I happen to hate her for another reason, at the moment."

"What's that?"

For a moment Daphne didn't want to tell. She looked very angry. Then she whispered, "She gave me a *doll* for my birthday."

"Oh," said Anastasia, feeling sympathetic. *"Oh."*

"You see? Revenge is definitely in order. Listen, we'd better get back. But I'll call you tonight. I'll get your phone number from Grandmother. And we'll plot something fiendish. Really sinister. I'm very good at that."

Anastasia had no doubt of that. But she liked Daphne. "Okay," she said, and grinned.

"Now," whispered Daphne, as she opened the door, "be careful when you pass stuff at lunch. Stand up

56

*straight*, or your bosom will fall in again, and I don't know if I can rescue you a second time. You're on your own, kid."

"Thanks," said Anastasia, and she headed for the kitchen, where Mrs. Fox was waiting.

# 5

Daphne called that very evening. By then, Anastasia was back to her normal appearance. She had ridden home, put her bike into the garage very quietly, watched from the back yard until she was certain her mother wasn't in the kitchen, and then crept as stealthily as a spy through the back door and up the back stairs to her third-floor room.

"Hi!" she had called from her room, after she had taken off her mother's bra, thrown the pantyhose into her wastebasket, wiped off the eye make-up, and brushed the powder out of her hair. "I'm home!"

"Hi there!" Her mother's voice came from the second floor. "How did it go?"

"Better today," Anastasia called back. "And I worked five hours, so I'm twelve-fifty less in debt!"

"Can I come up?" asked Sam's little voice from the foot of Anastasia's stairs.

"Sure. How was your visit to nursery school?"

Thu-dump, thu-dump, thu-dump. Sam's sneakers came up the stairs carefully, and he appeared in Anastasia's room, grinning. He was still holding Volume One of the encyclopedia.

"I can read." Sam beamed.

"Liar," said Anastasia.

"Look," said Sam. He put the book on her bed and turned to the section that he loved, the section with the airplane pictures.

Meticulously he inched his chubby finger along the lines of print until he came to the word "airplane."

"Airplane," he said solemnly. "That says 'airplane.'"

"Right. It does."

"Now look." His finger went along the lines again until he found the same word a second time. "Airplane."

"Right," said Anastasia.

"Everyplace it says 'airplane,' I can read it." Sam turned the page and his finger searched the lines. "Airplane," he pointed out triumphantly. "The lady at the school showed me."

So he hadn't been humiliated. Anastasia was glad. Two and a half was too young to be humiliated, actually.

Sam closed the book happily. "When nursery school starts for real, I'll take Volume Two. Then I can learn to read 'boat.' Volume Two has boat pictures in it."

"Don't they have things to play with at the nursery school? Blocks? Swings? Toy trucks? Didn't they show you those things?"

Sam thought, with his thumb in his mouth. "Yeah," he said after removing his wet thumb. "But those are for the babies. I'm only going to do books."

Anastasia groaned. Sam was such a weird brother. Probably he would be admitted to Harvard when he was nine. Probably he would still be wearing Pampers.

Later, at dinner, he wanted to bring Volume One to the table. He wanted to read "airplane" while he ate.

"No," said his mother. "Absolutely not. You can't read the encyclopedia with food on your fingers. It's against the rules of this house."

Sam's face puckered up, and he began to whimper.

"I have an idea," said his father. "Here, we'll set your highchair aside and put you on a real chair. And you can sit on Volume One to make you high enough."

Sam thought about that. "Okay," he said. He pushed another chair to the table and put his encyclopedia volume on it.

"Hold it," said his mother. "Your pants aren't wet, are they? No wet diapers allowed on the encyclopedia."

"Against the rules of the house?" asked Sam.

"Right. Against the rules of the house."

Sam felt his overalls. "No," he said triumphantly. "Not wet."

He sat on top of the thick volume, with his legs dangling. "Now I can only read 'airplane,'" he said. "But when I can read 'boat' I'll sit on two books. When I can read all the words, I'll be up to the ceiling."

"If you ever *ever* wet your pants on those books," said his mother, "I won't forgive you."

"I won't," promised Sam, swinging his legs cheerfully.

"I met a girl today," said Anastasia, "whose parents forgive absolutely everything. Probably if she burned their house down, they would forgive her."

"No kidding," said her father. He was carving a chicken.

"Even if she melted her father's Billie Holiday records, he would forgive her," said Anastasia pointedly.

"He sounds like a very strange sort of person," said her father as he passed her a plate of chicken. "Certain things are unforgivable in my book."

"My book," murmured Sam happily, and stroked Volume One.

"He's not strange," said Anastasia. "He's the minister of the Congregational Church. That's why he forgives everything."

Her mother passed the mashed potatoes. "The Congregational Church? That's right in the next block. It's that pretty brick church on the corner, Anastasia. The rectory's next door."

"No kidding! Hey, that's neat. I have a new friend who lives in the next block!"

"I'm not sure," said her father, "that I'd be in favor of a friend who would melt her father's Billie Holiday records."

"*Dad*, I didn't say she had. Or that she was going to. I just said that *if* she did, he would be very forgiving. Unlike other people's fathers."

"Well," said her father, "I may not be a minister, but I hold some things sacred. Original recordings by Billie Holiday are one."

Anastasia sighed. She was sorry she had brought up Billie Holiday. She hadn't meant to melt the records, anyway. She had simply stacked them on the radiator.

"What does it mean, hold things sacred?" asked Sam, with his mouth full of chicken.

"That you love them dearly," said his mother.

"That you respect them enormously," said his father, who seemed to be sulking a little bit, remembering his Billie Holiday records.

"That you wouldn't ever do anything to harm them," said Anastasia, reaching for a little piece of chicken skin. "Unless, of course, it was an absolutely unavoidable accident," she said meaningfully, looking at her father, "and then, of course, you shouldn't be held responsible."

Sam sucked his thumb dreamily for a moment. "I hold my airplane book sacred," he said.

✦

When the phone rang, after dinner, Daphne Bellingham didn't even say hello when Anastasia answered. She said instead, " 'Vengeance is mine, saith the Lord,' " in a sinister voice.

"What?"

"It's a quotation from the Bible," Daphne explained, giggling. "I know lots of Bible stuff because I've gone to Sunday school every Sunday since I was born, practically."

"Oh. I don't go to Sunday school. My parents said when I grow up I can choose whatever religion I want. I'm thinking of becoming a Buddhist."

"I think you have to be a vegetarian if you're a Buddhist," said Daphne. Then she giggled again. "But that would be okay. I notice you like deviled eggs."

"*Daphne.*"

"Sorry. I won't ever mention it again, honest. Anyway, I've been thinking about vengeance. I'm making a list of possible revenges on my grandmother. Can you come over? Where do you live?"

Anastasia told her.

"We're practically neighbors! Come on over. It'll take you about two minutes to get here. We're the brick house right next door to the church. There's a Nazi swastika mowed into the front lawn. I did it when I was supposed to cut the grass yesterday. My father forgave me, of course. But I have to mow it out tomorrow."

Anastasia promised her parents she'd be home by nine, and she went upstairs to change her clothes. She had already changed her clothes when she came home from work, but she didn't think ordinary jeans and shirt would be appropriate for visiting crazy Daphne Bellingham. She thought she should wear something outrageous.

Trouble was, she realized when she poked through her closet, she didn't own anything outrageous. Once she had wanted to buy a tee shirt that said BOOGIE TILL YOU PUKE. But her mother had said no. Actually, what her mother had said was no, absolutely not, not under any circumstances, over my dead body, that is final, the answer is No.

It had sounded fairly definite, so Anastasia had given up on the tee shirt. But now she wished she had it.

"Mom!" she called down the back stairs. "I don't have any clothes at *all!*"

"That's odd," her mother called back. "I didn't notice that you were nude at dinner."

Typical. It was tough to get sympathy from a mother. Anastasia finally pulled on her Mona-Lisa-with-a-mustache sweatshirt, some old jeans with paint on the knees, and a pair of sneakers.

"See you at nine," she told her parents, and grabbed a peach to eat on the way. "Night-night, Sam. I'm glad you learned to read 'airplane.'" Sam was sitting on the kitchen floor in his pajamas, reading his encyclopedia again. He blew her a kiss.

❖

Daphne's house looked quite ordinary from the outside. Brick and square, with shutters. Anastasia liked her own house better, with its odd porches and unexpected shapes, and the tower bedroom, which was hers. The only thing unusual about Daphne's house was the swastika in the lawn, and even that was barely noticeable, and also very crooked.

"Look!" cried Daphne, when she opened the front door. "How do you like them?"

"Like *what?*" asked Anastasia. Daphne was wearing bright red lipstick. It went way outside her own lips, like a clown's mouth.

"My Joan Crawford lips, of course," said Daphne. "And my Joan Crawford shoulders."

Anastasia looked more closely. She had been so startled by the lips that she hadn't noticed the shoulders. Daphne had put something inside her sweatshirt shoulders so that she looked like a football player.

"What do you think? If I can find some platform shoes, will I look just like Joan Crawford, or not? The shoulder pads are made of my father's ski socks."

"I guess it's okay. The mouth looks kind of like a clown, though."

"Yeah, I was afraid of that. I tried to make a crimson gash. Well, win some, lose some. Come on up, and I'll wipe it off. I'm bored with it already, anyway."

Inside, Anastasia could see that the house was very proper, very pretty. Furniture that matched, and no dust. Her own house was not as pretty but much more interesting, and messier.

But Daphne's room was different. The walls were painted black, and there was a huge obscene poster of two dogs tacked up between the windows. There were clothes all over the floor; Anastasia recognized the yellow and white dress that Daphne had worn to her grand-mother's luncheon lying in a pile with sweaters and jeans and underwear. On the unmade bed was a brand-new, expensive doll, with its clothes removed, staring with blue glass eyes at the ceiling. A kitchen paring knife had been plunged into its chest.

"I murdered the doll," said Daphne, grinning as she wiped off her Joan Crawford mouth and dropped the Kleenex on the floor.

"Did your parents *let* you paint the room black?" asked Anastasia.

"Of course. They let me do anything I want, provided it doesn't harm anyone. They're very big on not harming anyone."

Anastasia picked up the striped dress and hung it over the back of a chair, on top of a pair of shorts. "I like this dress," she said.

"Keep it. You can have it," said Daphne.

"Thanks," said Anastasia, a little embarrassed, "but my parents wouldn't let me. They'd kill me if I gave my clothes away."

" 'Faith, Hope, and Charity,' " said Daphne, " 'and the greatest of these is Charity.' Bible again."

"They'd *really* kill me if I accepted charity. Even a dress from" — she looked at the label — "Saks Fifth Avenue."

"Big deal. My grandmother gave it to me. I'm going to cut off the bottom and make it into a tee shirt, if you don't want it. My parents won't mind."

"Where are your parents, Daphne?" Anastasia realized suddenly that the house was very quiet. "And don't you have any brothers or sisters?"

"They're at a meeting. Or choir practice or something. They'll be home later. And no, no brothers or sisters. That's why I'm spoiled rotten."

"I have a dumb little brother," said Anastasia. "So I'm not spoiled rotten. It must be fun, though, to be spoiled rotten." In a way, she envied Daphne. But the black walls of the bedroom bothered her. They made her feel claustrophobic and depressed.

"Yeah, I guess it is. Here. Here's my list I've been making, of revenges. Some of them are just crazy, like putting poison in her iced tea. Some others are okay, like planting poison ivy in the rose garden, but I think it's too complicated. It probably wouldn't grow till next summer. What do you think about releasing a whole jar full of bees in her bathroom or something?"

"No. She might be allergic to bee stings. Anyway, we don't want to hurt her. You already said you weren't into hurting people."

"What exactly do we want to do to her?" asked Daphne, chewing on her pencil eraser.

"Well, there's all sorts of practical-joke stuff. Like once my brother, Sam, put my goldfish into my mother's cup of tea."

"I don't have a goldfish," said Daphne.

"I do, but you can't use him. He's been through enough. He's come so close to a nervous breakdown that now I'm seeing to it he leads a very quiet sort of life," said Anastasia.

"Anyway," she went on, "I don't think we want just a simple practical joke. She humiliated me by making me be a maid. Did she humiliate you by giving you a doll?"

"Yeah. *Really*."

"So. We have to humiliate her somehow."

"You know," said Daphne thoughtfully, "for someone to be humiliated, something has to happen in front of other people. Like all those people were there today, *looking*, when she gave me that doll. And you have to be a maid in front of everyone."

"Yeah, that's right. There have to be other people," said Anastasia, remembering what her mother and father had described about their humiliations. Other people. Other people *laughing*.

"Anastasia," said Daphne slowly, beginning to smile, "I am getting an idea. The perfect idea. The absolutely perfect humiliation for my grandmother. It's brilliant. It's so brilliant you won't believe it. It's —"

Anastasia interrupted her. "I'll believe it, Daphne. But hold on a minute. Could we go out in the yard or something? Frankly, these black walls are driving me crazy. If you want to know the truth, Daphne, I think your room is kind of sick."

"Yeah, you're probably right. I only did it to bug my parents. And now it's boring to have a black room. Maybe I'll paint it yellow next week. Come on down on the porch, and I'll get some lemonade. Hey, I know where my father keeps the vodka. Do you —"

"*No*, Daphne."

68

"Just asking." Daphne shrugged and grinned.

They sat on the screened back porch and sipped lemonade. Outside it had gotten dark. Somehow the dark of the night sky wasn't the same as the awful black walls of Daphne's room. It felt cooler here, healthier, and much more sane, Anastasia thought.

"Okay," said Daphne, when they were settled in the porch chairs, "here it is. The absolutely brilliant, absolutely foolproof, Krupnik and Bellingham Revenge and Humiliation Plot. Ready?"

"Ready," said Anastasia. "Atcher Service," she added.

"Okay. My grandmother is giving a big party next week."

"Oh, *no*," Anastasia said. "Probably she'll ask me to help serve." She groaned, thinking of herself in a maid's apron again.

"Well, it's a really big deal. It's to raise money for some charity. People have to donate a hundred dollars to some orphanage or hospital or something — I forget what — in order to get an invitation to this party. So a whole bunch of rich people are coming. And there'll be society reporters from the papers there. And an orchestra. And it's formal. Black tie."

"What does black tie mean?"

"Formal, dummy. Tuxedos."

"Gross. My father would never wear a tuxedo for a million dollars."

"Well, snobs like to wear tuxedos. And this party will be all snobs. Except . . ." Daphne started to giggle.

"Except what?"

"Well, the invitations have all been sent. But there was a batch left over. I guess my grandmother couldn't think of enough rich snobs to send them to. And I know where the leftover invitations are!"

"So?"

"So, I'm going to steal some. Maybe about twenty. And I'm going to send them to some other people."

"Like who?"

Daphne was roaring with laughter. "You haven't lived around here long enough. But I know all the so-called undesirable people in this town! There's an old drunk who sleeps on the sidewalk near the barber shop . . ."

"I've seen him! He's *awful!*"

"Right. Then there's a nutty lady who walks around over by the town park all the time, carrying a bag full of dog food. She wears about three pairs of stockings on top of each other. Gray, so her legs look like Babar the Elephant's."

Anastasia was giggling. She was beginning to get the picture.

"Then, let's see, there's all that low-income housing on the other side of town. I'll distribute a few over there. And there's a group home for deinstitutionalized psychotics, on Haverford Street."

"Group home for *what?*"

"Deinstitutionalized psychotics. Crazy people, but they're not dangerous, so they don't have to be in an institution anymore. I'll give them some."

"Daphne," said Anastasia slowly, "you know, we're

really not being fair. All of those people have problems. But it isn't fair to call them undesirable."

"*I* don't call them undesirable. I *like* them. I think they're the most interesting people in town. I even like that grubby old drunk. But my grandmother will think they're undesirable. And she's the one we want to humiliate, right?"

"Right." Actually, it was beginning to shape up as a terrific plan.

"There are a couple of guys who hang out in the park and smoke dope all the time. One of them was in jail once, I think, for selling drugs. I'll invite them."

Inside the house, the telephone rang. It rang a second time.

"Daphne, aren't you going to answer the phone?"

Daphne shook her head. "It'll just be for my parents. Let it ring."

"You're weird, Daphne. You're really weird," said Anastasia. She got up to go answer the telephone. But by the time she found it, after the fifth ring, there was no one on the other end.

"It's almost nine. I have to go home, Daphne," she said when she went back to the porch.

"Listen, don't worry about a thing. I'll get the invitations and I'll distribute them. They won't even have your fingerprints on them."

"Daphne, is this against the *law?* Could we get arrested?"

But Daphne just laughed. "Thou shalt not sweat it," she said.

Something was wrong at home. Anastasia could tell when she turned the corner. All the downstairs lights were on, and if something wasn't wrong, all the downstairs lights wouldn't be on. Her father was always yelling about the electric bill.

Then her heart sank. There was a police car in the driveway.

How could the police know *already* about the revenge she and Daphne were plotting?

I'll deny everything, she thought. Even if they put lighted matches under my fingernails. I'll say I never met Daphne Bellingham in my life.

They have to read me my rights, she thought. I'm entitled to a lawyer. I won't say anything that can be used against me.

It was an *accident* that I dropped the thing down the garbage disposal. And I've already paid back $17.50 of it.

Anastasia tried to think of every bad thing she had ever done. Surely her mother wouldn't have noticed yet that one pair of pantyhose was missing. Anyway, her mother wouldn't call the police about one lousy pair of pantyhose.

And the Billie Holiday records were two whole years ago. She shouldn't have reminded her father about them. But still, even though it had made him sulk at dinner, thinking about the Billie Holiday records, he wouldn't have called the *police*.

Terrified, she opened the back door.

"Anastasia!" said Mrs. Stein, their next-door neighbor.

What on earth was Mrs. Stein doing in their kitchen at nine P.M.? Mrs. Stein never went out at night. She had all her favorite TV shows to watch. She even liked the summer reruns.

"Sweetheart," said her mother, coming into the kitchen. "I tried to call you at Daphne's, but no one answered. You must have been outside. But I knew you'd be home in a few minutes. Thank God you're here."

Her mother's eyes were red. Anastasia could tell that she had been crying.

"What's wrong?" asked Anastasia in a small voice. Her stomach felt funny. She would confess, she knew. They wouldn't have to put the matches under her fingernails. She would tell everything: the plot, the pantyhose, even all the way back to the cupcake she had stolen when she was nine. If only her mother wouldn't cry.

"There's been an accident," said her mother, and put her arms around Anastasia.

"WHERE'S DAD?" asked Anastasia. "WHAT'S HAPPENED TO DAD?"

"Dad's okay," said her mother. "It's Sam. Dad's at the hospital with Sam. The police are going to take us there."

Later, Anastasia could barely remember the ride to the hospital. It seemed like a blur, or a dream. But she remembered her mother holding her hand and telling her what had happened.

They had put Sam to bed, with his ragged security blanket, which he always took to bed, and with his encyclopedia volume. He hadn't even wanted a bedtime story. He just wanted to read "airplane" to them once more, and then he kissed them good night, and they turned off his light and went downstairs.

Later — much later — her parents were in the living room, reading, when they heard a crash.

"Sam fell out of bed, right, Mom?" asked Anastasia, holding tightly to her mother's hand. "Dumb old Sam. He was fooling around with his crib, and he fell out of bed. He probably broke his arm or something, didn't he, Mom?" Funny, how when you wanted someone to laugh and say "Yes, that's right," you talked on and on, not giving them a chance to say it because secretly you were scared they wouldn't say it, but would say something else that you didn't want to hear.

And finally her mother squeezed her hand back and said no. Sam had apparently gotten out of his crib and had taken his airplane book over to the window — they didn't know why, but they thought maybe he had wanted to look into the sky for airplanes — and when he leaned against the screen it had broken, and Sam had fallen from the window.

Anastasia's stomach felt sick. The *window*. That was practically like the Empire State Building. Sam's window was very high. If they had only never moved from the apartment where they used to live — their first-floor apartment in Cambridge — if they had never moved to this enormous house — if only . . .

"Did it hurt?" she asked in a small voice. "Did he cry?"

"Sweetie," said her mother, "he was unconscious. We think his head hit that tree stump, where the dead elm tree had been taken down."

There was something else Anastasia wanted to ask, but she couldn't make her voice say the words. The police car was pulling up to the hospital entrance. Anastasia was still holding her mother's hand, and someone guided them in and put them in an elevator, and doors closed and doors opened, and suddenly she saw her father, sitting in an ugly green plastic chair, with his head down, looking at the floor. He looked up when he heard them, but he didn't smile; he just stood up, with his face sad and puzzled, and he reached out his arms.

Anastasia ran to him, and she began to cry. She made her voice say the words, and she asked the question, but it was the most terrible question she had ever asked.

"Daddy," she sobbed, "is our Sam going to die?"

# 6

No, they told her, but she didn't believe them. Sam is not going to die, her father told her, but she didn't believe him, even though he had never lied to her, not ever.

She cried and cried, and she didn't care that her face was red and her hair was messy and her glasses were falling off because tears made them slippery.

Then a nurse said it too, that Sam wasn't going to die, but she didn't believe the nurse, because nurses always said stuff like penicillin shots don't hurt, which was one of the most blatant lies in the whole world.

She cried because they had called her at Daphne Bellingham's, and Daphne hadn't answered the phone. She cried because she had called him old dumb Sam, and it wasn't true: he was smart, and he was young, and he was the only brother she had, and she loved him more than anything, and now she was sure they were all lying and he was going to die.

Once — more than once: *often* — she had hidden his blanky just to make him mad, just to tease him. She cried because she kept remembering that.

They all kept saying it to her, and she kept not believing them. But finally a doctor came through a doorway, wearing the same kind of operating room clothes that doctors on soap operas wear, and he said it, too, that Sam wasn't going to die, and when he said it, her parents began to smile. And then she believed it, because of the smiles.

Then she was able to stop crying, at last. The nurse gave her a little gray cardboard box of hospital tissues, and Anastasia blew her nose about a thousand times, and cleaned her glasses, and then she was able to listen to what the doctor was saying, because the inside of her head had stopped making crying noises.

"Your boy had a depressed skull fracture," the doctor said to Anastasia's parents, and he pointed to his own head to show them exactly where it was on Sam's, "and that's why we had to take him to surgery. But he's going to be just fine. At his age he'll heal in no time. You'll have him back home, oh, probably in a week or less."

"Can we see him?" asked her mother.

"Well, he'll be sound asleep for a good while. You folks may as well all go home and get some sleep yourselves. But if you want to wait twenty more minutes or so, you can peek at him while they wheel him to the recovery room. They'll be bringing him right along through here."

"Can we give him this?" asked Anastasia's father, and he held up Sam's ragged yellow blanky.

The doctor looked startled. "What *is* it?" he asked.

"His security blanket."

The doctor grinned. "Sure. Put it on the stretcher with him when they bring him out. Then he'll have it when he wakes up."

The doctor turned to leave. "Sometimes," he said, "I could use one of those myself," and he chuckled at Sam's blanky, nodded his head in response to their thank-yous, and went back through the door.

Anastasia, her mother, and her father, all sat down on the ugly green plastic chairs. Her father took his pipe out of his pocket and began to fill it with tobacco.

"I suppose they'll hand me a pamphlet about smoking if I light this in here," he said guiltily.

But there were ashtrays overflowing with the remains of other people's cigarettes. The Krupniks were the only ones in the waiting room. But Anastasia could tell that a lot of people had been there, worrying, that day. She wondered who they had been, and if they had all leafed through the same wrinkled *People* magazines on the table, and she hoped that they had all been as lucky as her family, and as lucky as Sam. She wondered if some of them had cried, and if the nurses had given them tissues.

Sometimes, when they had to kill time, like in a dentist's waiting room, or on a boring drive someplace, she and her mother played a game they had invented. Her father would never play; he said it was demented. The game was called Choices. "If you had a choice," it always began. They tried to think of the most terrible choices they could for each other, and it was against the rules not to choose. The worst one was one that her mother had given her: If you had a choice, would you eat liver at every meal for the rest of your life, and you would live to be ninety-seven, or would you stand naked in Lord & Taylor's main window for two hours on a Saturday afternoon?

She had tried, when her mother asked her that one, to narrow it down a little. To make it easier. Would the liver be *raw?* No, her mother said; it could be cooked. Could you wear a ski mask over your face in Lord & Taylor's window so that no one knew who you were? Well, said her mother, okay. You could wear a ski mask.

Even then, it was an impossible choice.

Now she began to pass the time, while they waited to see Sam, by asking herself: If you had a choice. But all of the choices centered on Sam.

If you had a choice, she said to herself, would you have leprosy, and your nose would have to be amputated, or would you let Sam die?

Leprosy, she told herself instantly. Nose and all.

Well, she said to herself: If you had a choice, would you marry that jerk Robert Giannini, and also never wash your hair for the rest of your life, and also join the Ku Klux Klan — or would you let Sam die?

I would do all that, she told herself, so that Sam wouldn't die.

I would *even*, she realized suddenly, eat liver *raw* three meals a day, and also stand in Lord & Taylor's window naked, *without* a ski mask, before I would let Sam die.

But he isn't going to, she thought happily.

Then, suddenly, there he was, being wheeled past by two nurses, who stopped briefly so that they could all look down at him. He was sound asleep; and his head was bandaged; and there was a needle in one of his arms, going to a tube that went up to a bottle hanging on a rack. But none of that mattered. He was still Sam, still old dumb Sam, and he was okay. Her father gave the blanky to the nurse, who tucked it in under Sam's limp little hand, and then they wheeled him away.

In the car, going home, Anastasia leaned against her mother. She was exhausted.

"Mom," she said sleepily, "I was thinking, at the hospital, and I decided that if I had a choice, I would eat liver raw . . ."

"Shhhh," said her mother, stroking her hair.

"And," she murmured, "I would marry Robert Giannini, and I would have my nose amputated, and join the Ku Klux Klan . . ."

"Mmmmm," said her mother.

"I forget the rest, but I would do it all, just for old Sam."

"Me too."

"Even the Lord and Taylor's window. I'd even do that, without a ski mask."

Her mother chuckled. "Of course you would. We all would. But we don't even have to think about that. Old Sam is going to be okay."

"You know what *I* was thinking, in there, while we waited to see Sam?" asked her father suddenly.

"What?"

"I was thinking what a weird injury he has. A depressed skull fracture. Can you imagine a *cheerful* skull fracture?"

They couldn't. But thinking about it made them smile, and they decided they would tell Sam about it. When he woke up. When he was okay. Tomorrow.

✻

"Anastasia," said her mother, after she hung up the phone the next morning, "the doctor says Sam is awake and doing just fine. And we can go to see him. But they have a rule about visitors. No one under fourteen."

Anastasia slammed down the dish towel that she was using to dry the breakfast dishes. "That's crummy! That's absolutely *crummy!* Everyone in the whole world is conspiring to get me! It's the one day I don't have to work, because Mrs. Bellingham is having people come to clean all the rugs and she's afraid I'll get in their way — which is idiotic — but I had the whole day free, and I was going to go and read to Sam, for Pete's sake. I was going to go to the library and get books about airplanes and take them to the hospital to read them to old Sam. And now they say I can't do that unless I'm *fourteen?* My own, my *only* brother, and some jerk has made a rule that I can't even read to him when he has a depressed skull fracture? That's not fair! It's crummy!"

She picked up the dish towel and slammed it down again. It wasn't very satisfying to slam a dish towel. A dish would have been better. But the dishes they had used for breakfast were her favorites — yellow, with white flowers on them.

Her mother looked angry, too. "You're right, Anastasia. Sam would *want* to see you. Probably if you didn't come he would start to cry, and run a fever . . ."

"And get a stomachache. It would be terrible for his health."

"Absolutely. It would be detrimental to Sam's entire recovery if you couldn't visit him. That is the *stupidest* rule!"

Dr. Krupnik appeared at the door to the kitchen. "What on earth is going on in here? You people are shouting and slamming and stamping your feet. You made the needle jump on the stereo."

Anastasia and her mother explained the hospital's rule.

"For heaven's sake," said Anastasia's father, "a rule like that is so dumb, it deserves to be broken. You're tall for your age, Anastasia. We'll just pretend you're fourteen. If they question us at the door I will swear a solemn oath, on pain of death, that you are fourteen years old."

"But Dad," said Anastasia, startled, "it would be a lie. Your whole philosophy of life is always to be honest."

"What's the date?" asked her father.

"August nineteenth."

Her father stood in front of the refrigerator, very straight and tall, with his hands at his sides. "On this date," he announced, in a loud, speech-making voice, "August nineteenth, Myron David Krupnik, Ph.D., honors graduate of several distinguished institutions of higher learning, member of the Authors Guild, Incorporated, vice-chairman of the English Department at Harvard University, noted author of several milestone volumes of poetry, contributor to the Civil Liberties Union and the Museum of Fine Arts, and general nifty person, declares that he has changed his entire philosophy of life. Drum roll, please."

Anastasia grabbed the frying pan that she had just dried, and beat on it solemnly with a wooden spoon. Her mother made some trumpet noises into the plastic funnel top of the coffee pot.

"Thank you," said Dr. Krupnik, and they stopped. "My *new* philosophy of life," he announced, "allows for the occasional posing of a five-foot, seven-inch, twelve-year-old girl as a fourteen-year-old girl, for the emergency purpose of cheering up her little brother, in the face of an idiotic bureaucratic rule."

He bowed. Anastasia and her mother applauded. Dr. Krupnik left the kitchen.

Maybe, thought Anastasia, it would help if I borrowed a bra again, and took some pantyhose, and . . .

No, she thought. Absolutely not. Her own philosophy of life, she decided suddenly, was never, under any circumstances, ever, to go anywhere again wearing a pantyhose bosom. You just could never predict when someone might ask you to pass a tray of deviled eggs.

✿

When they stopped at the library on the way to the hospital, Anastasia found all sorts of airplane books. *All About Airplanes. Conquering the Sky. Flight Through the Ages,* which opened with a picture of Icarus and his wax wings, melting when he flew too close to the sun. She checked it out because it had some wonderful photographs of jets at the end, but the picture of Icarus made her feel funny, because it made her think of Sam, falling. For a minute she wished that Sam had taken up some hobby other than airplanes. But what if he had taken up submarines? Probably he would have drowned. What if he had become interested in animal training? Somewhere he would have found a wild rhinoceros and been eaten up.

She shuddered. Well, her father had spent the whole morning fixing the screens on all the upstairs windows. At least Sam would never fall from his window again. And from now on, she told herself, she would keep a very careful eye on her brother *all the time* so that he wouldn't have any more accidents, ever. She planned to be the very best sister in the whole world.

And she would start by being a wonderful hospital

visitor. She planned to sit by Sam's bed and say soothing things to him, wiping his forehead with a damp cloth now and then, reading to him in a soft voice, and saying, "There, there," now and then when he whimpered with pain.

Maybe, in fact, she would go to nursing school, or even medical school, when she grew up. If only they wouldn't make her wear those white stockings. She really hated the white stockings that nurses wore.

But Anastasia's image of Sam the Invalid faded even before she saw him. She could *hear* him when they were still outside in the hall approaching his room. Not because he was whimpering feebly with pain. He was singing, in his loudest voice, "The monkey he got drunk, and sat on the elephant's trunk . . ."

He stopped singing when he saw his family. He grinned, waved, and said, "Hi! Did you bring me anything?"

The nurse who was in his room grinned also, and said, "Hi, there. You have quite a boy here. His repertoire of songs beats anything I ever heard at a fraternity party!"

Sam's mother went to the bed and kissed Sam's little face where it poked out beneath the turban of bandages. So did his father. Sam wiggled and made a face. He didn't like being kissed.

Anastasia thought about kissing him, but she just squeezed his feet through the covers, and said, "Hello, old Sam."

"It's okay to squeeze my feet," said Sam. "But don't squeeze my arm, because I have ivy on my arm."

Good grief, thought Anastasia. His brain has been damaged.

"You have *what*, Sam?" asked her mother.

"Ivy," said Sam. He pointed with one finger to the needle in the back of his other hand. A tube ran from the needle up to a bottle hanging on a metal stand.

"Oh." Mrs. Krupnik laughed. "An IV."

"That's what I said," said Sam with satisfaction.

"That's how they feed you, Sam, until you get a little better," his father explained.

"Yep. They feed me poison. It's my poison ivy machine."

Anastasia groaned. Sometimes Sam was impossible.

*

Later, back at home, the telephone rang.

"Anastasia? Willa Bellingham here. I've tried to reach you several times today."

"Well, I wasn't home, Mrs. Bellingham, because my little brother had a very serious acci——"

But Mrs. Bellingham interrupted her. "The rug cleaners have just left, and I am completely dissatisfied with the job they did. It is simply impossible to find conscientious workers these days."

"I try to be conscientious, Mrs. Bellingham," said Anastasia pointedly, and as politely as she could. But it was hard to be polite. She was furious. Mrs. Bellingham had interrupted her in the middle of telling about Sam's accident. Mrs. Bellingham was an insensitive creep. She didn't have the slightest interest in anyone else's problems. All she cared about was her stupid Oriental rugs.

Secretly, Anastasia hoped that someday a huge, un-housebroken dog would visit Mrs. Bellingham's house. Hah. So much for the Oriental rugs.

"Yes," said Mrs. Bellingham. "Of course you do. Now I would like you here tomorrow at ten, promptly. I'm giving a large party next week and there's a great deal to be done. I won't be home because I have my volunteer work to do. Mrs. Fox will give you your instructions."

Good grief, thought Anastasia. Probably the silver all needs to be polished again. She groaned silently, and calculated quickly in her head. She would have paid back her debt to Mrs. Bellingham in just seven more hours. Then she could quit.

But in a million years she didn't want to miss that party next week. She wanted to *be* there when Mrs. Bellingham was humiliated. She decided she wouldn't quit until after the party. School would be starting the week after that, anyway.

"All right, Mrs. Bellingham," she said.

"You'll be here *promptly* at ten?"

Anastasia sighed. "Atcher service," she said.

Rachel and Gloria were washing all the slipcovers in the house. There seemed to be about three million slipcovers. But Rachel and Gloria didn't seem to mind. They trudged back and forth to the washing machine and dryer and the ironing board, and they were quite cheerful. They called "Hi!" to Anastasia when she arrived. Anastasia had been a little worried that they might comment about her bosom, but they didn't seem to notice that it had disappeared.

Neither did Mrs. Fox, who was very busy making lists. She sat at the kitchen table, writing long lists of foods for the party, and she had ball-point pen marks on her lips, because she kept chewing on her ball-point pen.

Please don't ask me to polish silver, thought Anastasia. Please.

And it worked.

"Books," said Mrs. Fox, when Anastasia asked her what she should do. "In the library. Dust all the books." Then she nibbled at the ball-point pen again. Her lips were turning quite blue, like a creature in a horror movie. It was a rather interesting effect, and Anastasia thought briefly that maybe if she became a writer someday she would write a novel about a fat housekeeper who secretly became a werewolf at times, and maybe ate raw liver out of the refrigerator. Thinking about it made her stomach feel queasy.

But working in the library was fun. It was a medium-sized room that opened off the front hall, and all four walls were lined with bookcases. In the center there was a large mahogany desk. Probably Mrs. Bellingham sat at that desk and counted her money.

Probably she sat there and wrote her will.

Probably, thought Anastasia uncomfortably, she would disinherit her granddaughter if she knew what Daphne was up to.

There was a photograph of Daphne in the study, a color photograph of Daphne looking happy and wind-blown, wearing a blue sweater, somewhere with ocean in the background. It was in a silver frame.

The smiling Daphne in the photograph didn't look like the sort of person who would hate her own grand-mother.

In fact, until she had met Daphne, Anastasia had never known anybody who had hated her own grandmother. There had been times when Anastasia had gotten *mad* at her grandmother, but that wasn't the same. She had always loved her. Now that her grandmother was dead, she had her grandmother's wedding ring, which she kept in a small leather box. Sometimes she wore it to bed, because she thought that it might make her dream about the person she would marry. It hadn't worked yet, but it might, sometime.

Jenny MacCauley always went to her grandmother's house for Thanksgiving and Christmas, and her grandmother always made a miniature pumpkin pie just for Jenny.

Craig Robishaw had told her once that his grandmother had taken a ride on his trail bike, without even wearing a helmet.

Steve Harvey's grandmother lived in England, and when he had gone to visit her there, she hadn't made him go to museums or anything, but had gotten him a ticket to a rock concert.

Why was Mrs. Bellingham such a crummy grandmother?

Or — thought Anastasia suddenly — why was Daphne such a crummy granddaughter?

Anastasia took a rag from the bundle Mrs. Fox had given her and began to dust books. The books in Mrs. Bellingham's study weren't your ordinary Literary Guild Alternate Selection, best-seller sorts. And no trashy novels. These books were all leather-bound, deep blues and reds, with gold printing on the covers. Classics, thought Anastasia. First editions. The kinds of books her father would love.

Her father had once said that he would kill for a first edition of something by Joyce James. Or maybe it was James Joyce; she couldn't remember.

Probably the book her father would kill for was right here in Mrs. Bellingham's study. She knew he was exaggerating, though. Her father would never kill anything. Maybe a cockroach. Nothing else.

Probably Mrs. Bellingham never even read any of these books. Some of their pages were stuck together, proof that they'd never been opened.

Her father would read every one, she thought sadly. Life just wasn't fair. She had never really wished before that her family was rich. Now she wished it for a minute, just so that her father could have these books.

She had dusted a complete set of novels by Henry James. Anastasia didn't know who Henry James was, but she had heard her father speak about him. Her father taught a course in Henry James at Harvard. She had once wondered how someone could spend an entire semester just teaching about one author. If she ever had to take a whole course in, say, Nancy Drew, she would be so bored by the second week that she would probably drop out of college and become a waitress.

Now she could see that Henry James, whoever he was, had written more books than the author of Nancy Drew. Now *that* was an accomplishment. Poor Henry James. He had to spend all his time writing in order to write so many books. He probably never went out for pizza or anything. He couldn't possibly have any social life; there wouldn't be time. She wondered if Henry James had ever been to a movie or a disco. Probably he was *old* by now and had never had any fun in his whole life. He must have been sitting at a typewriter for fifty years.

Probably he was Mrs. Bellingham's age.

Probably he would enjoy meeting Mrs. Bellingham, since she had bought all of his books. He wouldn't have to know she'd never read them.

I could get my father, thought Anastasia, to tell Mrs. Bellingham the plots of the books. Then she could pretend she'd read them. A lot of kids at school did book reports just by reading the inside flaps of the covers and maybe the chapter headings. My father could fill old Bellingham in on the plots; then we could invite Henry James to dinner, and Mrs. Bellingham, and it might be the start of a big romance. She could say stuff like, "Henry, I loved that last book of yours" — Anastasia glanced at a title — "*The Turn of the Screw.*" Then old Henry could twirl his mustache, if he had one, and say, "Thank you, Willa. May I take you to the movies on Friday?"

But then Anastasia made a face. It would never work. With a title like *The Turn of the Screw,* old Henry's novel was going to be about hardware. Hardware or sex. She was quite certain Mrs. Bellingham wasn't interested in either subject.

Anyway, why should she drum up a romance for Mrs.

Bellingham, who had never done anything for her except humiliate her?

She had another idea. There was a fountain pen on the desk. What if she wrote, inside the cover of *The Turn of the Screw*, "To my dear Willa, with fond memories of the passionate night we spent together. Henry James"?

She could do it in *lots* of books.

"Willa, dearest: I will never forget the week in the hotel room in Paris. Fondly, Scott Fitzgerald."

Or: "Willa, my love, you are the inspiration for all of my work. Charles Dickens."

Anastasia giggled, thinking about it. But she didn't do it. Not that she cared anything about Willa Bellingham's reputation. But she cared about the books.

Carefully, she dusted the last of the Henry James and set it back on the shelf. She started on the complete set of Virginia Woolf.

Suddenly the door to the study flew open, and there was Daphne, grinning.

"Greetings from the Cat Burglar!" Daphne said. Then she whispered, "I'm here to steal the invitations. They're in her desk, and I knew she wasn't home today. She spends half her time out doing dumb charity work. Giving her money to poor people or something."

Daphne opened a desk drawer, took out a handful of thick, engraved cards, and stuck them into her backpack. "There, that'll do it. I'll make the deliveries over the weekend."

"Let me know how it goes," said Anastasia.

"I will. I'll call you. Where were you yesterday? I kept calling, and no one was home."

Anastasia explained briefly about Sam's accident. Daphne's blond eyebrows furrowed, and she looked concerned.

"Gee, that's awful. Is he going to be okay?"

"Yeah. He's doing fine."

"You really love him, don't you, Anastasia? I can tell from the way you talk about him."

"Love Sam? Of course I love Sam. He's my *brother*, for Pete's sake!"

"I wish I had a little brother," said Daphne wistfully. Anastasia was startled. It was the first time that she had seen Daphne being anything other than flippant, funny, or sarcastic.

Then Daphne's mood changed. "Hey," she said, "I have to go. I told Mrs. Fox I'd come by to pick up a sweater I left here. *Voilà!* The missing sweater!" She laughed, and took a sweater out of her backpack.

"I'll call you!" she said, and left the study.

Anastasia picked up a volume of Virginia Woolf and began to rub the soft leather with her dustcloth.

That was weird, she thought, when Daphne said she'd like a little brother. Daphne hates her whole family. Why would she want one more person to hate?

She doesn't, Anastasia thought suddenly. Daphne wants someone to love.

❖

It seemed lonely at the dinner table, with just the three of them and no Sam. Anastasia's mother had spent the afternoon with him at the hospital.

"Tell us everything," said Anastasia. "How he looks, and what the doctor said, and everything."

"How soon can he come home?" asked her father. He had had to teach a class that afternoon. "I really miss him. I even miss changing his diapers."

"Well," said Mrs. Krupnik, "I guess it falls into the category of Good News, Puzzling News, and Terrible News."

"Start with the Good," said Anastasia. "And if the Terrible is really terrible, I don't want to hear it."

"Good News: he can come home on Monday. He's recovering just fine. The nurses say they've never seen anybody bounce back as quickly as Sam has. He's sitting up, doing puzzles, looking at his books — he really loves those airplane books you brought him, Anastasia."

"Good! I'll go over tomorrow afternoon and read to him, if I get out of work in time."

"You said there was *puzzling* news?" asked her father.

"Yes. When I got there, he was having lunch. They've taken out his IV and started him on regular food. So he was sitting there with a tray of food in front of him. They'd given him soft-boiled eggs."

Anastasia burst out laughing. "Oh, gross! The one thing Sam hates more than anything else in the world! Soft-boiled eggs! He always makes fake throwing-up noises when he even *sees* a soft-boiled egg!"

"Well," said her mother, "that's part of the puzzling

thing. There he sat, with a nurse's aide helping him, and he was eating his soft-boiled egg. I didn't want to create any problems, but I was so startled that after he was all finished, I said casually, 'Gee, Sam, I sort of remembered that you didn't much care for soft-boiled eggs.'"

"Understatement of the world," Anastasia pointed out. "What did he say?"

"He said, 'Mrs. Flypaper told me to eat everything so that I'd get well quick.'"

"Who's Mrs. Flypaper? The nurse's aide?"

"Well, that's what I thought. So I said, 'Are you Mrs. Flypaper?' to her, but she said no, her name was Miss Cameron. Then I asked Sam who Mrs. Flypaper was, and he just grinned and said, 'She's my friend.'"

"What kind of friend could ever get Sam to eat a soft-boiled egg?"

"I don't know. I asked all the nurses, but none of them knew of anyone named Mrs. Flypaper or anything that even sounded like Mrs. Flypaper. When the doctor came in, I asked *him*, but he didn't know who it could be."

"It doesn't sound terribly important, Katherine," said Anastasia's father.

"Well, it wouldn't be. But I started thinking, what would make a child eat something that he never in his entire life has eaten voluntarily? Even when he was an *infant* he'd spit soft-boiled eggs out all over his high-chair tray! And on top of that, what would make a child say that someone who apparently doesn't even *exist* had convinced him to eat soft-boiled eggs? Especially if that child had had a serious head injury?"

"Good grief," said Anastasia. "Brain damage."

"Right," said her mother. "That's exactly what I started thinking. And I suggested it to the doctor. But he said they've done all sorts of tests, and Sam's brain is functioning just fine. In fact, Sam is the brightest two-and-a-half-year-old they've ever seen in the pediatric ward."

"Of course he is," said Anastasia's father smugly.

"But then the doctor and the nurses and I were all starting to wonder about the mysterious Mrs. Flypaper and the soft-boiled eggs. So they called in a child psychiatrist."

"A junior shrink!" said Anastasia.

"Right. So the psychiatrist came in — a woman named Dr. Cunningham — and she talked to Sam for a long time."

"What did she decide?"

"She said he's the brightest two-and-a-half-year-old they've ever had in the pediatric ward."

"Big deal," said Anastasia. "We already knew that. What about Mrs. Flypaper?"

"She said Sam has invented an imaginary friend."

"A *what?*"

"Well, she said Sam has been through a very stressful situation . . ."

"Big deal," said Anastasia a second time. "He fell about a million feet from a window, landed on his head, had an operation, and woke up in a hospital bed with ivy in his arm. *I* could have told you he's been through a stressful situation, and I never went to psychiatrists' school!"

"Let me finish. She said that very often, particularly with very bright children, they will invent an imaginary companion to help them get through the fear and loneliness and pain of hospitalization. So Sam invented an imaginary friend named Mrs. Flypaper."

"You'd think he would have chosen a better name," said Anastasia. "*Mrs. Flypaper*. That's so dumb."

"Well, dumb or not, Sam invented her, or him, or it, and she convinced him to eat soft-boiled eggs."

"That's weird."

"Well, I told you it was puzzling."

"Katherine," said Anastasia's father, "you've given us the Good News and the Puzzling News, but —"

"I don't want to hear the Terrible News," said Anastasia firmly. "May I be excused? I'm full."

"No, stay here, Anastasia. You've got to hear the Terrible News, especially if you're going to visit Sam tomorrow. You may as well be prepared."

"My stomach hurts. My stomach hurts already, and I haven't even heard the news yet."

"They've taken the bandages off Sam's head," said her mother. "The doctor said the incision will heal faster if it's exposed to air."

"I hate that word, *incision*. Does it look awful?"

"No, actually it doesn't look all that bad. It's very neat, with little even stitches."

Anastasia's father said, "I'm surprised that you can even *see* the incision, with all of Sam's curly hair."

Her mother looked miserable and didn't say anything.

"His hair!" said Anastasia suddenly. "It's his *hair*, isn't it? His curls. What have they done to Sam's curls?"

But she knew, even as she asked. It *was* Terrible News.

"They shaved his head," said her mother in a sad voice.

Her father sighed, and then started to laugh. "Good grief," he said. "That's not the end of the world. It'll grow back!"

But Anastasia knew how her mother felt. She felt the same way. "Dad," she said unhappily, "you don't understand."

She asked her mother fearfully, "How does he *look?*"

Her mother's eyes were filled with tears. But she was biting her lip, too, and Anastasia could tell that she didn't know whether to laugh or to cry. So she did both. The tears ran down her cheeks. But she was chuckling when she answered the question.

"He looks like Kojak," she said.

# 8

It was true. A miniature Kojak, wearing seersucker pajamas printed with pictures of Mickey Mouse.

Anastasia flinched when she saw Sam. But she didn't say a word about his shaved head. She had decided, while riding her bike to the hospital, that she wouldn't, no matter how gross it looked.

She remembered how terrible she had felt one morning, back when they lived in Cambridge, when her best friend, Jenny, had greeted her with "Hi, Anastasia! That's an awful mosquito bite on your forehead. It looks just like advanced acne."

It really was only a mosquito bite. But after Jenny said that, Anastasia was self-conscious all day. She tried to comb her hair over her forehead. She sat with her hand over her forehead as much as possible, until her sixth-grade teacher asked whether she had a headache, and when she said no, told her that she looked like Balboa discovering the Pacific Ocean. And showed her a picture of Balboa, with his hand over his forehead, discovering the Pacific.

Hah. Probably old Balboa had advanced acne.

So Anastasia was always very careful not to point out anyone's physical flaws, because she knew from experience how awful it made them feel.

So she said, "Hi there, Sam!" just as if he didn't look like Kojak at all.

But to her surprise, Sam said, "Hi! You can call me Baldy!"

Dumb old Sam. He wasn't old enough to be self-conscious yet.

"Well," she said uncomfortably, "I guess I'll just call you Sam, the way I always do."

Sam shrugged happily. "Okay. But Mrs. Flypaper calls me Baldy. Mrs. Flypaper says I look like Bald Eagle the Indian chief."

Imaginary Mrs. Flypaper. Anastasia was still puzzled by that. What good was an imaginary companion who said you looked like Bald Eagle the Indian chief?

Well, obviously it made Sam feel okay about the way he looked. What if, when she had had the mosquito bite on her forehead, and Jenny had made that obnoxious remark, Anastasia had had an imaginary companion — a Mrs. Flypaper — who had said, "Don't worry about it. It just looks like a mosquito bite. No big deal"?

No. It wouldn't have worked for her. She needed a *real* friend to say that, not a made-up one.

But if it worked for Sam, okay.

"I'll bring you a feather next time I come, Sam, and we can make an Indian headdress for you."

"Okay," said Sam cheerfully.

"We really miss you at home."

"Yeah," said Sam.

"Last night when Mom was setting the table, she forgot and set four places. One for you."

Sam giggled. "I eat on a tray. Sometimes Mrs. Flypaper comes when I'm eating."

And makes you eat soft-boiled eggs, thought Anastasia. Weird.

"Where does Mrs. Flypaper come *from*, Sam?"

Sam looked puzzled. "I don't know."

"When you come home on Monday, will Mrs. Flypaper come with you?"

Sam looked startled. "No," he said. "Mrs. Flypaper lives *here*."

Well, that made sense. Sam needed his imaginary companion only while he was in the hospital. Just like the shrink said.

"Would you like me to read to you?"

"Yeah. About airplanes."

So Anastasia climbed up on the high hospital bed and read to Sam from one of the library books she had brought him. She skipped the Icarus section. She had a feeling that it would be dangerous to read it to him.

Old dumb Sam, he might start trying to build a set of wings.

After a while, Sam snuggled down in his pillow and fell asleep. Anastasia kissed the top of his bald Kojak head, whispered, "See you tomorrow, Bald Eagle," and tiptoed out of his room.

*

She didn't have to be home for dinner for another hour, so Anastasia rode her bike to Daphne's house. Funny, she thought as she rode, how quickly this town had begun to feel like home. She rang her bicycle bell as she rode past the library, and waved in case Mr. Mason, the librarian, was looking out the window. He and she had become good friends, even though she thought he was overly strict about the number of books you could check out at a time.

She rang her bell again, and waved again, as she passed the Senior Citizens' Center. Sometimes when she was bored at home, she stopped in there and played checkers or gin rummy with the senior citizens. They didn't seem to mind that she wasn't a senior citizen herself.

She waved to Mr. Mastrolucci at the Gulf station where her father got gas. Then she waved to Gladys at the Clip 'n Curl Beauty Salon. For a while she had been mad at Gladys, because Gladys had refused to bleach Anastasia's hair platinum blond. But then she had realized that Gladys was right. Anastasia didn't really have a platinum blond face. Or figure. Maybe she would when she got older, especially if she got contact lenses and stopped being so skinny.

She also waved at a lady she didn't even know, a lady who was walking a dumb-looking dog with droopy ears. The lady looked surprised. The dog didn't.

Then she turned into Daphne's driveway, and there was Daphne, sitting on the front steps with a cat on her lap.

"Hi, Daph! You said you'd call me, and you didn't! What are you doing?"

"Picking fleas off the cat." She let go of the big gray cat, who looked relieved, jumped off Daphne's lap, and ran away into a thick clump of bushes. "I *did* call you. I called you this morning, and your mother said you were at work. And I called you this afternoon, and your father said you were at the hospital. Boy, your parents really keep track of you, Anastasia, like a couple of jailers."

"No, they don't. They just like to know where I am. I like to know where they are, too. If you don't keep your eye on people, they fall out of windows and stuff."

"How's your brother?"

"He's okay. I read him a couple of books." Anastasia decided not to tell Daphne that Sam was bald all of a sudden. It seemed too personal. And Daphne might laugh.

"Guess what? I did it," said Daphne.

"Did what?"

"Delivered the you-know-whats."

"No kidding! How many?"

"Twelve. That was all I took. My grandmother didn't notice they were gone, did she?"

"She wasn't home this morning. She was out doing charity again, I guess. But Mrs. Fox didn't say anything. Anyway, they're all so busy cleaning the house and the dishes and the furniture and everything, they're not even thinking about the invitations. Who did you give them to?"

"Everybody I told you I would."

"The drunk who sleeps by the barber shop?"

"Yep. He was sitting there on the sidewalk, nodding over a bottle of Gallo's rosé. I gave him one."

"What did he do?"

"He read it. Then he stood up, bowed, and said, 'My dear, I am decidedly honored.'" Daphne did a pretty good imitation of a staggery bow. Anastasia giggled.

"How about the lady who carries the dog food around?"

"Yeah. I found her sitting on a bench near the police station, mumbling to herself. I gave her the invitation, and she stuffed it into her bag and went on mumbling."

"Probably she won't even read it."

"Of course she will. I said to her, 'Aren't you even going to read it?' And she got all mad and yelled at me that of course she was going to read it, she always reads everything, she's read the complete works of Proust fourteen times, and when there's nothing else to read she reads the telephone book. Then she started mumbling again."

"Who else?"

"The potheads in the park. I gave them two. And two to the deinstitutionalized psychotics."

Anastasia counted. "That's six. Who got the other six?"

"Well, then I walked over to the low-income housing. You know what my grandmother calls that housing project?"

"What?"

Daphne stood up, stuck her nose in the air, pinched her lips tight together, squinted her eyes, until she looked amazingly like Willa Bellingham, and said, in a throaty voice, "The Habitation of the Great Unwashed."

"Daphne!" Anastasia was shocked. "That's terrible! Being low income doesn't mean being unwashed!"

"It does to my grandmother. Unless you wash with imported lilac soap from England, you're unwashed. She says that every time we drive past that project: the Habitation of the Great Unwashed." She did her Willa Bellingham imitation again. Anastasia was impressed.

"You know, Daph, you'd be a really good actress. I can't think of any professional actress who could do that imitation as well as you."

"Bull. Jane Fonda could. Vanessa Redgrave could. Maybe Bo Derek couldn't, though."

"Is there a Dramatic Club at school?"

Daphne shrugged. "I suppose so. I'm only going into seventh grade, the same as you, so I don't know much about the junior high. But there was a Dramatic Club where I went to sixth grade."

"I bet you got the lead in all the plays, didn't you?"

106

Daphne made a face.

"*Didn't* you?" asked Anastasia again.

"No," said Daphne finally. "I didn't belong to the Dramatic Club."

"Why *not?*"

Daphne didn't say anything. She looked around, into the bushes where the cat had hidden. "Here, Scooter!" she called.

"*Daphne.* Listen to me. You *have* to join the Dramatic Club in junior high, because you'll get the lead in everything. Then after you finish high school you can go to New York, to the Academy of Dramatic Arts or something, and then Hollywood will find you, and you'll be a star. You'll win Oscars, and write your autobiography, and all that. I can tell you have a lot of talent. I bet not even Lily Tomlin could do that imitation of your grandmother. Honest. Now tell me *why* you wouldn't join the Dramatic Club!"

Daphne stood up again, and looked down her nose at Anastasia. "Because it met after school," she said in a haughty voice. "And I was not available after school."

"Why not?"

Daphne's shoulders sagged, and she spoke in her own voice, but it sounded sad and angry. "I told you, Anastasia. I am a *troublemaker.* I was always in detention after school."

She turned and went up the steps to her house. "It doesn't leave much time for extracurricular activities," she said sarcastically. Then she went inside and slammed the door.

Boy, thought Anastasia, as she rode her bike home. I thought I was worried about Sam. But all he has is a depressed skull fracture. Daphne is really the one to worry about. Daphne has a depressed *brain* or something.

# 9

Anastasia was making pancakes. She often made pancakes for the family on Saturday mornings. But this Saturday it wasn't much fun, without Sam there. Sam liked pancakes shaped like rabbits or snowmen. Her parents didn't.

"You want a snowman, Mom?" she asked, raising the bowl to pour the batter into the pan.

"No, thanks. Just round will be fine."

So Anastasia made a boring round pancake and served it to her mother.

"Dad?" she asked. "How about a rabbit? I can really make good ears when the pan's nice and hot."

But he made a face. "Frankly, your pancake rabbits make me cringe. They make me think I'm slicing the

Easter bunny. Just do me a round one like the one you did for your mother."

"I could put raisins in it," Anastasia suggested.

But he made an even more hideous face. "Spare me the raisins. A round, plain, unadorned pancake, please."

Adults were so boring about food. Anastasia wished for the millionth time that Sam were home. Sam even let her put food coloring in his milk.

She served her father an enormous round pancake, made herself a halfhearted snowman, and sat down to eat.

Boring, boring, boring Saturday morning. I bet breakfast isn't boring at Daphne's house, because Daphne can do those great imitations, Anastasia thought. If Daphne were here, my parents would be holding their sides from laughing, instead of just reading the newspaper.

Anastasia decided to try doing an imitation. She decided to do a waitress routine, since she was making pancakes anyway.

She chewed a wad of imaginary gum, and said, "Pancakes are on special today. Only a dollar sixty-nine. Can I give you folks another order of pancakes?"

"No, thank you," said her mother, and folded the newspaper into quarters so that she could begin the crossword puzzle. "You could pour me some more coffee, though."

"Me too," said her father without looking up from the paper, and pushed his cup over.

Anastasia glowered and poured both of her parents some coffee.

She chewed harder on the imaginary gum, scraped the frying pan noisily with the spatula, and said, in her waitress voice, "Tips sure are lousy in this here diner."

Her father cleaned his glasses with a paper napkin. "Katherine," he said, "do you have page thirty-six? I need the rest of this article on the defense budget."

"It's on the chair," said her mother, and pointed to the section that contained page thirty-six.

Rats. It hadn't been a *great* waitress routine, but surely it had deserved some polite applause, at least.

She decided to borrow Daphne's imitation of her grandmother. She *knew* that was funny.

"Have you guys ever noticed," Anastasia asked casually, "that over on the other side of town there's a low-income housing project?"

"Mmmmm," said her mother, filling in a word in the crossword puzzle. She looked at the word, frowned, and erased it.

"Yes," said her father, as he turned a page of the paper. "I drive past it when I go to work. I've forgotten what it's called. Hazelnut Estates, or something."

"No," said Anastasia's mother, looking up. "It's Hazelwood. Hazelwood Acres, I think, Myron."

Perfect, thought Anastasia. If she had been writing dialogue for a play, she couldn't have written it any better, to lead up to her great line.

"Actually," she said, "what it's called is" — and she drew up her shoulders very stiffly, pinched her mouth into a sour expression, and looked down her nose — "the Habitation of the Great Unwashed."

But no one laughed. Both of her parents were looking at her. And there was an ominous silence.

Her father, in the terrible voice he reserved for the most awful occasions, broke the silence by saying, "Did I just hear you say what I *think* I heard you say?"

"Repeat that, please," said her mother, staring at her. "I want to be certain I heard you correctly, Anastasia."

Good grief, thought Anastasia. *Big* trouble. She looked at her plate, where one bite of a pancake snowman still lay soggily in some syrup.

"Thehabitationof thegreatunwashed," she finally repeated, mumbling miserably. "I was only —"

"*That*," interrupted her father angrily, "is the stupidest, most uneducated, mindless, bigoted remark I have ever heard you say!"

"But —" began Anastasia.

"*Snobbish*," said her mother. "I can't believe it. You, of *all* people, turning into a *snob!*"

"What I meant was —"

"What you *said* was 'unwashed.' Is that correct? Did I hear you correctly?" asked her father.

"Yes." Anastasia sighed. "You heard me right. Unwashed. But I was only —"

"Do you have any understanding of what low income means?" her father demanded.

Anastasia looked him in the eye. Now *she* was mad. "Dad," she said, "I myself am low income. So far this week, at work, I earned forty dollars, out of which I had to pay thirty-five for a bockle, so that my take-home pay was five dollars. Plus the extremely low-income allowance that you give me. Don't talk to *me* about understanding poverty, for Pete's sake. I *live* it."

"And do you consider yourself 'unwashed'?" Her father said the word with distaste.

"No. My jeans are unwashed, but —"

"And do you consider *poor* to be synonymous with *unclean?*"

Anastasia could see that she was doomed to lose a war she hadn't intended to start. "No," she said.

"Or the underprivileged to be lacking in human dignity?"

"No. Definitely not."

Her mother had gone back to the crossword puzzle. "It was just a thoughtless remark, Myron," she said.

Unfortunately her father didn't have a crossword puzzle, and he had apparently finished the article about the defense budget. He set the newspaper aside.

"You haven't ever seen where I grew up, have you, Anastasia?"

"You grew up in Boston," Anastasia said.

"I grew up in Boston. I also grew up in *poverty*. My mother, my father, my four brothers and I all lived in a four-room apartment." Her father stood up and took his plate and coffee cup to the sink.

Anastasia poked unhappily at the last bit of her soggy pancake. She didn't want it. But she didn't want to hear a lecture, either, about the millions of underprivileged people who aren't fortunate enough to have pancakes for breakfast. She gulped down the last bite.

"The bathroom was down the hall," her father said.

"We shared it with two other families." He rinsed his plate. Back at the table, her mother sighed and erased another mistake in the crossword puzzle.

Anastasia carried her own plate to the sink and held it under the running water. Her father watched her, meaningfully.

"We didn't have hot water," her father said. "My mother heated water on the stove."

Ho-hum, thought Anastasia. But she nodded politely.

"BUT WE WERE NOT UNWASHED!" said her father. "Can you get that through your head?"

Not if you yell at me, thought Anastasia. All I get through my head if you yell at me is an Excedrin headache.

But she nodded again. "Yessir," she said.

Dr. Krupnik stroked his beard. He looked more cheerful all of a sudden. "You know what?" he said. "It's Saturday. And it's a beautiful day. Let's go for a ride, Anastasia. I'll show you where I lived when I was a kid."

Anastasia stifled a groan. There was nothing she wanted to do *less* on a Saturday than take a trip down Memory Lane with her father. But she smiled sweetly, and said, "Sure, Dad."

I brought it on myself, she thought, and went to brush her teeth.

"Mom," said Anastasia, as her father got the car out of the garage, "up in my room, on my desk, is a big feather. Would you take it to Sam when you go to the hospital? I promised him."

"Sure."

Out in the driveway, her father honked the horn. Anastasia sighed. "He really knows how to ruin someone's Saturday," she said.

Her mother picked up the crossword puzzle again. "Good for you, Anastasia! *Ruin!* Four down. The clue was 'to devastate.'"

"Right. That's what I meant. He's completely devastated my Saturday." She went glumly out to the car.

"My father never had a car," announced Dr. Krupnik as he pulled into a Boston parking garage. "Never in his whole life did my father own a car. If he *had* owned a car, he would never have been able to afford six dollars for parking in a garage. Six dollars would have fed our whole family for a week, back in 1935."

Anastasia tried to look interested. Actually, she was bored stiff. Though she had never seen her father's childhood home before, she had heard all his dull poverty stories. Every twelve-year-old kid had, she was quite sure. Every twelve-year-old kid in the entire world had to listen to things like "When I was your age I walked five miles to school in my bare feet." Or, "When I was your age I had to milk twenty-three cows by hand before the sun came up, in the middle of winter." Or, "When I was a kid, all we got for Christmas was an orange and a pair of mittens." Probably even Rockefeller kids had to listen to things like that.

Anastasia vowed that when she had children she would never ever tell them what a deprived childhood she had had. That she had had to work as a maid when she was only twelve. That she had lived in a house with an old refrigerator that couldn't make reliable ice cubes. That she had never in her entire childhood been taken to Disneyland.

She looked around as they left the garage.

"Dad!" Anastasia said. "This is Quincy Market, for Pete's sake! I've been here before! I *hate* Quincy Market! It's all tourists! Did you live here when you were a kid? Did your father run a boutique or something?"

Her father looked at her in surprise. Then he looked around at Quincy Market: at the restaurants, art galleries, gift shops, pubs, and clothing stores. He began to laugh.

A middle-aged couple, each carrying a camera, glanced at Anastasia and her father, and frowned. Nearby, a young man with a scraggly mustache tuned his violin and began to play; someone tossed a coin into his violin case, which was open on the brick sidewalk.

"Of course I didn't live here. This wasn't even here when I was a kid. I mean, the *buildings* were here — you can see that the buildings are very old — but in those days, when I was a boy, this whole area was . . ." He stopped talking, scrunched his nose, moved aside to let a throng of tourists pass, and tried to think of the right word.

"The pits?" asked Anastasia, beginning to get the picture.

Her father grinned. "Yes. It was definitely the pits. Anyway, where I lived was over this way. Come on."

He guided her across a street, under an underpass — she could hear the cars zooming overhead — and onto the sidewalk in front of an Italian meat market. A burly dark-haired man wearing a white apron called to them from the doorway. "You want chicken? We got lotsa chicken parts on special today! Eighty-nine cents a pound!"

"No, thanks," her father called back. "Not today."

"Lamb chops?" the butcher called. "Loin lamb chops?"

But they were already around the corner. Anastasia's father was guiding her as he looked for street signs.

"Salem Street," he said, almost to himself. "If we go down Salem Street, and then turn right, I think . . ."

She trotted beside him, dodging the people. Children darted here and there, calling to each other. From upper windows women leaned, calling to the children. In store-front doorways, men stood, calling to the women in the windows.

One of the men called to Anastasia, "Hey, Blondie, you and your papa wanta pizza?"

Actually, Anastasia would have loved a pizza, as long as it didn't have anchovies. Anchovies always made her think of her goldfish. She had always suspected that un-sold goldfish ended up as pizza anchovies.

But her father was striding ahead of her, looking down side streets. She said, "No, thank you," politely to the pizza man and ran to catch up. "Maybe later," she called back, over her shoulder, but the pizza man was already calling to someone else.

From an open window above her somewhere she could hear familiar music. Anastasia looked up. A woman was reaching from the window, hanging diapers on a clothesline that stretched across to the next building. The music was coming from behind the woman.

"Dad," she said, pulling at his sleeve. "Listen. Someone's playing that opera that you always play."

He stopped walking, listened for a moment, and then looked up at the woman, who was snapping diapers straight as she pinned them to the line.

"Puccini, eh?" her father called. Ordinarily, Anastasia was grossed out when her father spoke to total strangers in public. But somehow it seemed okay here. The woman grinned down from her window and called something back to Dr. Krupnik, in another language.

He smiled, waved, and called, "*Ciao!*"

"Chow?" said Anastasia. "That sounds like a good idea. All these restaurants smell terrific."

"No: *ciao*. That's Italian. It's just a greeting."

Two little boys ran past, chasing each other, almost knocking over a woman pushing a baby carriage, and disappeared into a candy store. The woman with the baby called after them angrily and then turned to jounce her baby back to sleep. Anastasia couldn't understand what she was saying.

"Dad," Anastasia said, "*everybody's* speaking Italian!"

"It's their native language," her father explained. "They know how to speak English. If they were talking to us, they'd speak English. But to each other they speak Italian. Here: I think we want to turn down that next street. It's been so long since I've been back here."

They turned to the right, down a twisted, crooked street so narrow that she didn't see how a car could possibly get through. One had, though, and had parked, and it had a ticket that said VIOLATION, in big letters, on the windshield. Shabby buildings rose on either side and shadowed the street. Old women sat knitting, in lawn chairs, right on the sidewalk. Two men played checkers at a card table set up in a doorway; a dog by their feet yawned and scratched at a flea. Children scampered and giggled and chased each other. Babies cried; mothers scolded; a cat slept, unconcerned, in a window.

Even the graffiti spray-painted on the side of a building were in Italian.

"There it is!" said her father triumphantly, and he pointed to an undistinguished brick building on the corner. "Third floor rear!"

They climbed the three cement steps that led to the doorway, and peered inside. A row of metal mailboxes was attached to the wall. Anastasia read the names aloud: "Castelucci, De Luca, Ronzoni, Di Benedetto.

"It sounds like the cast of a Fellini movie," she said.

Then she looked around again, at the tiny street throbbing with life, at the children, the grandmothers, the cats, and dogs. She listened to the noises: doors slamming, radios playing, the shouting, arguing, laughing, singing. "As a matter of fact," she said, "being here is like being in a Fellini movie."

Her father grinned. "I love it," he said.

"I love it, too," Anastasia admitted. "I thought it

would be boring, coming here, but it isn't. But there's something I can't figure out, Dad. Were you *Italian* when you were a kid?"

He laughed. "Anastasia, do I *look* Italian?"

She studied his face carefully. A little chubby. Head bald on top; remaining hair red and curly, with some streaks of gray on the sides. Pink nose, with dents in it because his glasses had slid down a bit, the same way hers did when it was hot and her face got slippery. Curly beard.

"No," she said finally. "You don't."

"My parents came here from Czechoslovakia. This whole area, when I was young, was a place where immigrants from many different countries settled. My father came here first. Then, after he'd saved enough money, he sent for my mother."

"What about you? What about your brothers? Did she come alone, and leave you behind in Czech—— in Czech—— I can't say it."

"Czechoslovakia. No, no. We were all born right here. Third floor rear."

"Not in a *hospital?*"

"Hospitals were too expensive. I told you, Anastasia, my family was *poor*."

She cringed, waiting, but he didn't say anything about unwashed.

He was wrinkling his forehead, looking around, remembering. "My father was a tailor. At first he worked for someone else. But I don't know where that was. It was before I was born. By the time I came along, he had his own shop; it was around the corner and down about half a block."

He looked around the corner and down. But there was nothing except an Italian restaurant, a dry cleaner, and a pastry shop.

"Well," he said finally, "it's gone now, of course. But in the summer, when I wasn't in school, I used to carry his lunch down to the shop every day."

"Were there other people around from Czech—— from Czech—— Rats, Dad; I still can't say it."

"Czechoslovakia. Sure there were. Lots. A whole community. Some of them were even old friends from the same village back in the old country."

"Where did they all go? Why aren't they here now?"

"Let's walk, and we'll find a place to have some lunch." He put his arm around her shoulders, and they turned onto another street, walking slowly. "Where did they go? Different places, I guess. They all worked hard, and saved, and looked for good places to raise their children. I think they looked for places that reminded them of the old country. My mother and father eventually bought a little house farther out, where they could have a yard and my mother could have a garden."

"But he never ever had a car," Anastasia mused. "I thought everybody in the suburbs had to have a car."

"Nope. He could never afford a car. But he sent all five sons to college," her father said proudly.

"And then two of them died," Anastasia prompted him. "I remember you told me that."

"Right. My brothers Joe and Ben. Both of them killed in the war."

"That is *so* sad," said Anastasia. "When I thought *my* brother was going to die, I couldn't stand it."

"But there's still my brother George, in California."

"Uncle George. He and Aunt Rose always send me neat stuff on my birthday. An Indian necklace once, remember?"

Her father nodded. "And then, of course, there's Irving."

Anastasia groaned. "The doctor. He is so boring, Dad."

"Anastasia!"

"I'm sorry. But he is."

"I guess you're right. Irving was always boring, even when he was a kid."

"But you liked him anyway, didn't you, Dad?"

"Sure I did. I still do. He's my brother."

"Like me and Sam. Even when Sam is boring, I still like him," said Anastasia.

Her father began to laugh. "Anastasia, Sam is *never* boring!"

"True," she acknowledged. Then she said, "You know what, Dad? I know someone who hates her whole family."

"Extraordinary," said her father. "Extra-absolutely-ordinary. Unless her whole family are ax murderers or something."

"No. They're just your basic family types. They do some dumb things, though."

"We all do. I remember just last week I blew up at you because you used all the ice cubes and didn't put the ice trays back. That was a pretty dumb thing."

"Which was? Not putting the trays back? Or blowing up about it?"

"Both, in fact. But we didn't hate each other because of it. I think your friend must be just *pretending* to hate her family."

"Why would she do that?"

"Beats me. Hey, you hungry yet? Want some chow?"

"*Ciao!*" said Anastasia.

"*Ciao* to you, too!" said her father.

Two nuns walking past looked at them curiously, nudged each other, giggled, and walked on.

"In here okay?" asked her father. Anastasia nodded, and they entered a small Italian restaurant.

"I'm glad the Italians didn't scrimp and save and move away, like the Whatchamacallits," said Anastasia, after two mouthfuls of spaghetti. "I'm glad they stayed here."

"Well," said her father as he ate his antipasto. "Lots of Italians moved away to the suburbs, too. But some of them chose to stay here even after they could afford to move."

"They stayed because they liked it, I bet."

"Sure. They made it into something like a part of Italy. A little bit of Naples or Florence. It felt like home."

Anastasia slurped a long piece of spaghetti when she thought no one in the restaurant was looking.

"Dad," she said slowly, "I was really mad at you this morning."

He poked in his antipasto with his fork. "You want an anchovy?"

"Yuck," said Anastasia. "Blecchhh."

"A simple 'No, thank you' would be sufficient," her father said, and ate the anchovy himself. "I was pretty mad at you, too."

"I know you were. But the reason I was mad was that you didn't even give me a chance to explain."

"There isn't any explanation for bigotry," he said. "Not ever."

"I know that. I really do. But I wasn't even thinking about *what* I was saying. It was the way I was saying it. I was imitating Mrs. Bellingham. Mrs. Bellingham is so *awful*."

"You know," said her father, "I agree that Mrs. Bellingham did a pretty thoughtless thing when you applied for one job and she sort of tricked you into another. But on the other hand, Anastasia, I've decided that she's not such a bad person after all."

"Dad! She made me be a *maid!*"

"You didn't let me finish. I read in the local paper that she's giving a party next week. Did you know about that?"

"Did I *know* about that? Who do you think is going to be a maid at the party?"

He poked at the last bits of lettuce in his salad. "Oh. I see. Well, let's try looking at it in a different way, Anastasia."

Now Anastasia was getting mad. "There isn't any other way. No matter how you look at it, a maid is a maid is a maid is a maid."

"Not always. How about being a maid for a very worthy cause?"

Anastasia made a face. She couldn't think of a single cause worthy enough to justify Anastasia Krupnik's being a servant. A scullery maid. A slave.

"The paper said that it's a benefit. People are paying enormous amounts of money to go to that party," her father said.

"I know. A hundred dollars apiece," said Anastasia, almost smiling as she thought of the wonderful disaster that she and Daphne were going to cause.

"And all of that money," her father went on, "probably twenty thousand dollars, is going to go to the pediatric section of the hospital. The same place that saved Sam's life."

Oh, no. Oh, *no*. Anastasia's heart sank. Her heart sank and her stomach churned. A whole plateful of spaghetti began to *move* inside her stomach. She felt first hot and then cold. Her hands began to sweat.

"Holy Moley," she said under her breath. "Excuse me, Dad."

She ran to the ladies room. Four dollars and ninety-five cents' worth of spaghetti with sausages and mushrooms. Right down the drain.

# 10

It was too late. It was just too late, and Anastasia knew it, but she called Daphne anyway, on Sunday afternoon, after she had recovered from being sick.

She had thrown up four times on Saturday. Her parents blamed it on the sausage in the spaghetti. You could never tell, her mother said, what people put into sausage. She had heard rumors about dead cats and ground-up tennis shoes. Anastasia's father threatened to call the Board of Health, but he couldn't remember the name of the restaurant.

Anastasia knew it wasn't the sausage anyway. The sickness had started in her brain and her heart — and in her conscience — and had worked its way down, very quickly, to the sausage, which was an innocent by-stander.

By Sunday afternoon her stomach felt okay. But her conscience was terminally ill.

"Jeez," said Daphne on the phone, after Anastasia had explained, "there's nothing we can do now. I don't even know the names of any of the people I gave invitations to. The only thing I can think of is to call in a bomb threat so the party will be cancelled."

"No good. I think that's a federal offense. If we got caught, we'd go to prison. I'm already nervous enough about making friends in seventh grade. Imagine what prison would be like. I can't think of one single thing to say to a bank robber or an ax murderer."

"Anyway," Daphne pointed out, "we don't want the party cancelled. Then the hospital wouldn't get the twenty thousand dollars."

"Right," said Anastasia. "The party has to be held. But we'll have to try to keep it from being a disaster. Forget about humiliating your grandmother."

"Yeah. We'll just keep an eye on all the weird guests. Keep them from making awful scenes. If the drunk guy starts getting drunk . . ."

"Or the dope dealer starts trying to sell drugs . . ."

"Or if that crazy lady comes with her bag full of dog food . . ."

"We'll just ask them to leave," said Anastasia.

"Politely," said Daphne.

"But firmly," said Anastasia.

"And quietly," said Daphne, "so my grandmother never knows what's going on."

"Then the party will be a success," said Anastasia, beginning to feel relieved.

"And the hospital will get its money," said Daphne, "and we won't get into trouble."

"Daphne," said Anastasia, "I really wish we hadn't dreamed up this idea in the first place."

"I know the feeling," said Daphne. "I feel that way about most of my crazy ideas. Usually by then it's too late."

❊

Sam's homecoming on Monday was something of a disappointment to Anastasia. She had expected to meet the car when her mother drove in, to help carry Sam up to his bed, to sit there with him and read him stories, to feed him custard — maybe even soft-boiled eggs — and say soothing words. But she should have known better. Sam had been driving the nurses crazy for two days now with his high spirits, good health, and energy. Ever since his mother brought him the feather, he had worn it Scotch-taped to his bald head and had pulled Bald Eagle commando raids in the hallways of the pediatric ward. There had even been, the nurses told Anastasia's mother, a terrible collision involving a bedpan.

They all adored Sam, they said at the hospital. But they were awfully glad he was well enough to go home.

Now he climbed exuberantly out of the car, wearing his little blue jeans, with a baseball cap on his head, and carrying an armful of airplane books. So much for Anastasia's fantasy about having an invalid for a brother. The invalid came noisily through the back door, dropped his books on the kitchen floor, and demanded a SpaghettiOs sandwich for lunch.

Anastasia had seen too much of spaghetti in various stages of digestion lately. She didn't think she could survive watching a SpaghettiOs sandwich being eaten.

"Welcome home, Sam," she said. "I cleaned up your room for you."

"Did you mess up my stuff?" he asked.

"Nope." She had left a pile of blocks and a half-constructed castle on the floor, some mysterious Tinker Toy objects that might have been airplanes on his little table, and a long line of Matchbox cars running from one side of the room to the other. "I should have, though," she said. "You've messed up *my* stuff often enough."

Rats, thought Anastasia, and felt guilty. She had made a solemn vow that if Sam got well, she would never be mad at him again. Now he hadn't been home five minutes, and she had already made a grouchy remark. In her entire life, she thought, she had probably made at least four hundred solemn vows, and she had never been able to keep a single one of them.

I am definitely Lacking in Character, thought Anastasia.

Then and there she made a solemn vow that she would keep Mrs. Bellingham's party from turning into a disaster so that the hospital where Sam had been fixed up would get its twenty thousand dollars. Never before had she made a solemn vow involving so much money. This solemn vow she would keep, she thought, and the size of it would make up for the four hundred others.

Still, she was not about to watch Sam eat a Spaghet-tiOs sandwich. It was almost time to go to work, anyway.

"See you later, guys," she said to her mother and to Sam. "I'm off to wax the Bellingham antiques."

❀

By seven P.M. on Wednesday, the antiques were waxed, the rugs were shampooed, the books were dusted, the silver was polished, the caterers were busy in the kitchen with the food, and the orchestra was tuning its instruments on the terrace. Anastasia had been picked up at home by the chauffeur, because she wasn't allowed to ride her bike at night. Daphne was there, wearing a blue silk dress. There were no deviled eggs. Chinese lanterns were hanging outside, lighting the terrace and the gardens. A photographer from the newspaper was loading his camera with film, and in the study a bartender had set up a bar with so many bottles that it looked like the Ritz.

Mrs. Bellingham came down the staircase dressed in a flowing gown sewn with tiny pearls, and her hair piled on top of her head.

"Anastasia," she said. "You —"

"I know, Mrs. Bellingham," Anastasia interrupted. "I'm to pass the hors d'oeuvres, and ask people if they would like another drink, and pick up empty plates and glasses and take them to the kitchen. Mrs. Fox already told me."

Mrs. Bellingham smiled. "I'm sure she did. And I know you'll do everything perfectly, because you've been very conscientious about every job you've been given, ever since you began work. I'll miss you, after this evening."

Tonight was to be Anastasia's last night of work. School would begin next week.

"Could you stop by tomorrow, Anastasia, to be paid? Things will be so hectic this evening," Mrs. Bellingham went on.

Anastasia nodded.

"As it happens, dear, you interrupted me," said Mrs. Bellingham. "I wasn't going to tell you what to do tonight. I was going to tell you that you look beautiful. Very grown up."

"Oh," said Anastasia, startled. "Thank you." She was wearing her very best dress, new shoes, and tiny silver earrings. She had *felt* beautiful, at home, when she got dressed. Her mother and father had said that she looked beautiful. But it was kind of nice to hear Mrs. Bellingham say it. Parents always said stuff like that even when it wasn't true, so you couldn't entirely trust them. She smiled after Mrs. Bellingham, who had gone on into the living room to rearrange the cushions for the millionth time, and made the solemn vow again that she would keep the party from being a failure.

❖

Two hours later, the party was not yet a disaster. But Anastasia's nerves were. Things weren't going the way she had expected them to.

First of all, she hadn't been able to recognize any of the special guests that she and Daphne had invited. She had thought that they would be very visible because of their clothes. The invitation had said "black tie." She knew that, because Daphne had told her. That meant that the official guests — the rich guests — would be wearing tuxedos, at least the men would, and the women would be wearing evening gowns.

She had thought that it would be very easy to recognize the town drunk, in his stained and rumpled clothes. And the dog-food lady in her many layers of unmatched dresses and stockings. And the drug dealer in his ragged jeans.

But there was only one man wearing anything like jeans, and that was a tall, slender man in a denim jumpsuit with sequins decorating the pockets. Anastasia had thought for a minute that he must be the drug dealer, wearing his dressiest outfit, and that she should go over and (politely, firmly, quietly) ask him to leave, before he tried to peddle some marijuana, maybe to the mayor or something.

She had made her way over to where he was standing, pretending that she was going to offer him some mushrooms stuffed with crabmeat. But just as she approached, a gray-haired woman in a black satin dress swooped down on the man.

"Lester!" she had cried. "I've caught you at last! I

have a potential client I want you to meet!" She took his hand and pulled him over to another woman, who was sipping champagne.

Good grief, thought Anastasia. He's going to make a sale right here, practically publicly, right in front of a twelve-year-old maid. If my parents hear about this, I'll be killed.

"Darling," the woman in black was saying to the other woman, "this is Lester, the *best* decorator in Boston!"

"And the most expensive," said Lester haughtily as he shook hands.

Anastasia had leaned against the wall, unnerved. What if she had asked the best decorator — and the most expensive — in Boston, politely, firmly, and quietly, to leave? She felt sick to her stomach just thinking about it.

She had realized, then, that she must make her moves very, very carefully. She must be completely certain that she was kicking out the right people. But it was so hard to tell. Not all of the men were wearing tuxedos; some were in ordinary suits. The women were in all kinds of outfits, not just evening gowns; some wore strange pants — one was even in chiffon knickers — and some were wearing plain short dresses. Almost any one of them could have come from the low-income housing project. There was no way to tell.

And they were all ages. She had thought that she would recognize the guys who hung out in the park smoking pot — even if they weren't wearing their ragged jeans — because they were young. But there were many young people here. The most humiliating moment of the evening so far had been when a young man — college-student age — had politely asked Anastasia if she would like to dance.

In her entire life no one (except Robert Giannini, at a square dance once, and that didn't count. Robert Giannini, of all people. At a *square* dance, for Pete's sake) had ever asked Anastasia to dance. Now it was actually happening. And the guy was as handsome as a movie star. The orchestra was playing something romantic, and there was an almost-full moon. It was the worst moment of Anastasia's entire existence.

"I can't," she mumbled.

"You mean you don't know how? Come on, it's easy," he said, smiling at her.

"No," she said, agonized. "I mean I'm the maid." And she ran away.

Anastasia kept passing the endless trays of mushrooms, chicken livers, and cheeses, wondering what she should do. Suddenly she spotted, standing against the wall, someone who looked vaguely familiar. He was standing alone, wearing a very ordinary suit, apparently half asleep, drinking a drink.

She watched him. As she watched, he gulped down the last of his drink, set the glass on a table, and went to the bar for another. He came back to his place against the wall and stood there, drinking sleepily again. Anastasia was quite certain that she recognized him. But she had never seen him dressed in a suit and tie before.

He has to be the drunk who sleeps on the sidewalk near the barber shop, she thought. And if I don't kick him out, he's going to slump to the floor, sound asleep and *drunk,* and ruin Mrs. Bellingham's party.

I will be polite, she said to herself. And firm. And quiet. I will say, I'm sorry, sir, but you're going to have to leave now.

She rehearsed it in her mind. I'm sorry, sir, but you're going to have to leave now. I'm sorry, sir, but you're going to have to leave now.

But when she walked over to him, she didn't say it. Instead, she said politely, "Hello."

He stared at her for a moment, and then smiled. "You look familiar," he said, "I'm sorry, but I can't remember your name."

*That* was weird. She shouldn't look familiar to him. It was supposed to be the other way around. She recognized him because she'd seen him sprawled on the sidewalk. But he had never seen her. He'd always been asleep.

"My name is Anastasia Krupnik," she said, "and you look familiar to me, too." And she said to herself once more: I'm sorry, sir, but you'll have to leave now. But she couldn't make herself say it aloud.

"Krupnik," he said suddenly. "Of course. I should have remembered. You're Sam's big sister. How's he doing?"

Anastasia was stunned. How on earth did the town drunk know Sam?

"He's fine," she said, puzzled. "He has a scar on his head, but when his hair grows back you won't even be able to see it."

"Of course not," the man said, smiling. "I stitched it very carefully."

Then she knew. The man wasn't the town drunk at all. He was the surgeon who had operated on Sam.

She wanted to sink through the floor and disappear. What if she had actually said to him, I'm sorry, sir, but you'll have to leave now? What if she had taken his arm (firmly, quietly) and tried to propel him to the door.

"Excuse me," Anastasia said. "I have to pass food. I'm the maid."

Then she went to the powder room to recover. Daphne was just coming out. They looked at each other.

"Big trouble," said Daphne. "I just threw up."

"Why? Have you been drinking champagne or something?"

"No," said Daphne, but she looked stricken. "I just blew the whole thing. Ruined the party."

"I *almost* did, myself," said Anastasia miserably. "What did you do?"

"I've spent the whole last hour trying to figure out who is who. I couldn't even recognize the people I gave the invitations to."

"I know. I've been doing the same thing."

"And *finally* I thought I recognized one."

"Me too. But I was wrong."

"I bet you weren't as wrong as I was," said Daphne.

"I bet I was," said Anastasia. Sam's surgeon. Good grief. It made her cringe to think of it.

"I saw this man, and he looked familiar . . ."

"Yeah. I know."

"So I watched him for a while. And he was talking and talking, telling some long dull story with no point to it. Everyone around him was trying to be polite, but you could tell they were all bored and wishing they could get away from him. And I *knew* I'd seen him before."

"Yeah," said Anastasia sympathetically. "I know the feeling."

"Then I noticed that his suit jacket was buttoned wrong. You know, he had the wrong button in the wrong buttonhole, so it was all bunched up down the front. And there were other clues, too. He was wearing a Red Sox button in his lapel. Nobody in his right mind would wear a Red Sox button to a black-tie party, right?"

Anastasia groaned. "Right. So what did you do?"

"I went up to him and said very politely, the way we practiced, 'I'm sorry, sir, but you'll have to leave now.' "

"What did he do?"

"He just looked at me for a minute. *Everybody* looked at me. There was a hideous silence. Then he said" — Daphne drew herself up, tucked her chin against her neck, and imitated a deep, pompous voice — " 'Young lady, who do you think I am?' "

Anastasia groaned again. "What did you say?"

"Well, he *asked*. So I told him the truth, about what I thought. I said, politely and firmly . . ."

"And quietly?"

"Not quietly enough. Everybody heard me. I said, 'I think you're a deinstitutionalized psychotic.' "

"And he wasn't," said Anastasia. But she already knew that he wasn't.

"No," said Daphne, "he definitely wasn't."

"Who was he?"

Daphne took a deep breath. "He was the mayor," she said.

# 11

Anastasia woke the next morning with the sense that she had had a bad dream. Then she remembered. It hadn't been a bad dream at all. It had been real.

The mayor had sputtered and glowered and sought out Mrs. Bellingham to ask *who* this obnoxious child was. And it was Daphne.

Mrs. Bellingham had demanded an explanation from Daphne, who had excused herself and run to the powder room to throw up. That was when Anastasia discovered her there and heard what had happened.

They had talked briefly about the possibility of running away together, maybe joining a circus or something. Hitchhiking to Hollywood, perhaps, where

Daphne could achieve stardom with her dramatic talents, and Anastasia could be her manager.

But none of it seemed very practical, and besides, there was Mrs. Bellingham, suddenly standing over them.

"Anastasia," she said, "you can go on back to the party and continue your duties. I have something to discuss with Daphne."

It was her chance to flee. But she couldn't.

"Mrs. Bellingham," she said, "you may as well discuss it with me, too. Because I was just as involved as Daphne."

"It was my idea, though," Daphne pointed out.

"*What* was?" asked her grandmother. "What *is* going on? You two girls come with me right now into the study and explain this to me."

So they did. They had no choice.

Funny, though, that it wasn't too hard explaining what they had done. Daphne even got into being dramatic about it, imitating the lady with the bag of dog food and the drunk on the sidewalk receiving their invitations to the black-tie party. Mrs. Bellingham's lips twitched, as if she wanted to laugh.

The hard part — the *impossible* part — was explaining *why* they had done it.

"I was mad," said Daphne hesitantly, "because you gave me a doll for my birthday."

Mrs. Bellingham looked puzzled. "But it was a beautiful doll, Daphne," she said. "I bought it at —"

"Grandmother," Daphne interrupted angrily, "I'm *thirteen* years old."

"Mrs. Bellingham," Anastasia said so that Daphne wouldn't have to take all the blame, "I was mad, too. Because when I was looking for a job, I wanted to be a *Companion*, and you made me into a *maid* without even asking me."

"I see," said Mrs. Bellingham, and Anastasia could tell that she was *trying* to see. But also that she didn't, really.

There was a silence. Then Mrs. Bellingham said slowly, "Why didn't you tell me? Both of you. Daphne, why didn't you explain to me about the doll? And Anastasia, why didn't you come to me and explain your dissatisfaction? You were always so courteous and hardworking that I had no idea you were angry."

Anastasia thought for a minute. Then she said, "Because I was scared of you, Mrs. Bellingham."

And Daphne said, "Me too, Grandmother. I was scared of you."

Mrs. Bellingham looked startled.

Anastasia suddenly felt very, very sorry about the whole thing. Not because she had been caught. And not because the party had been ruined. But because Mrs. Bellingham looked so surprised and so sad.

"Well," said Mrs. Bellingham, "I think I'll have the chauffeur run both of you girls home. Anastasia, don't forget to stop by tomorrow for your money."

"Mrs. Bellingham, I don't think I deserve to be paid,"

said Anastasia. And she meant it. But it felt terrible, saying it. All of those hours of work for no pay.

"Nonsense. You worked hard, and you did a good job, even tonight. Come by about ten tomorrow morning."

"Grandmother," said Daphne, "I don't mind being sent home. In fact, I *want* to go home, because my stomach hurts. But what about the party?"

"What do you mean, what about the party? The mayor seems to have simmered down. The party will continue without your presence, Daphne."

"But Grandmother," Daphne said meekly, "all of the people that we invited are still out there somewhere. The dog-food lady, and the drunk, and the psychotics, and the low-income people, and . . ."

Her grandmother sighed. "Daphne," she said, "surely it is apparent by now that those people, whatever their problems, know how to behave at a party. Which is more than I can say for you at the moment."

Then she led both girls through the back hall to the kitchen door and instructed the chauffeur to take them home.

Anastasia lay in her bed and remembered it all. She felt awful. Even her goldfish wouldn't look at her. He swam with his tail turned toward her.

"Well, the hospital got its money, anyway," she said belligerently to Frank, the goldfish. But he only twitched his tail. He wouldn't turn around.

How humiliating, to be snubbed by your own goldfish.

After a while she sighed, got up, pulled on some old clothes, and went downstairs. Her parents were drinking coffee in the kitchen, and Sam was running a toy truck around the floor.

"Hi!" said her mother. "How was the party? You went to bed so fast last night that I didn't have a chance to ask you. You must have been exhausted."

"I was." Anastasia poured some milk over a bowl of Cheerios and began to eat. "The party was okay."

Someday she would have to tell them the truth about it. Not now, though. Maybe when she was thirty or something.

"I have to go over to Mrs. Bellingham's pretty soon and collect my pay."

Sam looked up from his truck. "Can I come?"

"No," said Anastasia. But then she began to think. Maybe it would help, having Sam along. Maybe Mrs. Bellingham wouldn't say too much if Sam was there.

"Well, maybe," she said. "Mom, may I take Sam with me? Did the doctor say Sam could go out?"

Her mother hesitated. "He can go out. But not on the back of your bike, Anastasia. It's too risky. We're supposed to keep him from bumping his head."

"*Mom,* I haven't had a wreck on my bike since I was *nine.*"

"I know. But still, it's just too dangerous."

"Well, I'll walk. It's only a mile or so. I'll take Sam in his stroller, okay?"

"Yeah," said Sam. "In my stroller! Can I go? Can I?"

"Well," said his mother. "Okay. If you're careful."

"I will be," said Sam. "I'll be careful. I told Mrs. Fly-paper I'd be careful."

143

Anastasia, her mother, and her father all groaned. They were sick of hearing about Sam's imaginary friend.

Sam just grinned and went off to find his Indian feather.

*

As they approached the gate to Bellmeadow Farm, Anastasia detached the feather from Sam's head.

"You can't wear that here, Sam," she said, "because I want the lady to think we're very respectable. I won't be able to explain to her about Bald Eagle. She wouldn't understand."

"Okay," said Sam agreeably.

"Now, when I introduce you to her, I want you to shake her hand. Okay?"

"Okay," said Sam.

"And say 'How do you do, Mrs. Bellingham.' Can you say that?"

Sam giggled. "How do you do, Mrs. Bellybutton," he said.

"SAM! Don't you dare! I'll clobber you if you say that! Now say it right."

"How do you do, Mrs. Bellingham," Sam said dutifully.

Anastasia pushed the stroller to the back door, lifted Sam out, and rang the doorbell. "Now, don't forget," she whispered to her brother.

Mrs. Bellingham came to the door herself.

"Good morning, Anastasia," she said.

"Good morning. This is my brother, Sam. Sam, this is Mrs. Bellingham." She watched Sam carefully to be sure he behaved properly.

"How do you do," said Sam, and held out his little hand. Then he looked up and stared at Mrs. Bellingham. His eyes widened. Anastasia nudged him. "How do you do, *Mrs. Bellingham,*" she reminded him in a whisper.

But he wasn't listening. He was grinning at Mrs. Bellingham. And she was grinning back at him.

"It's brave Bald Eagle!" she exclaimed, and reached down to pick Sam up. "Where's your feather, Chief?"

"Mrs. Flypaper!" cried Sam happily, and threw his arms around her neck.

*

Good grief, thought Anastasia. This is what I thought it would be like, being Mrs. Bellingham's Companion. Here I am, sitting in her study, like a real human being instead of a maid, drinking iced tea brought in on a tray by Mrs. Fox. And there's Sam, drinking orange juice out of a silver cup, which I won't have to polish.

And there was Mrs. Bellingham, stirring sugar into her tea with something that looked very like a bockle, and smiling like a real human being, too.

"You see, Anastasia," she was explaining, "I work as a volunteer in the pediatric ward of the hospital. I never know the children's last names, because I don't read their charts. That's why I didn't know Sam was your brother.

"All the volunteers wear pink smocks," she went on. "I wear a name tag on mine, but of course a lot of the youngsters aren't old enough to read . . ."

"*I* am," said Sam smugly. "I can read 'airplane.' "

"So some of the little ones just call me Pinky. It's easier to remember than Mrs. Bellingham."

"Mrs. Bellybutton." Sam giggled.

"*Sam!*" hissed Anastasia.

But Mrs. Bellingham was laughing. "Good old Sam," she said. "He doesn't like to do what everyone else does. When I suggested that he call me Pinky, he made a face . . ."

Sam scrunched up his nose and eyebrows. He stuck out his tongue. It was one of his standard yuck-I-don't-want-to-do-that faces.

"Right." Mrs. Bellingham laughed, watching him. "It was that face exactly. Then he said that he would call me Mrs. Flypaper. Don't ask me why."

"Because you made one for me," Sam explained. "You zoomed it across the room."

For a moment Mrs. Bellingham looked puzzled. Then she brightened. "The paper airplane! I made him a paper airplane!"

"Yep," said Sam. "A flypaper. I zoomed it right into your behind, remember?"

Mrs. Bellingham blushed. "I believe it was my *hip* you hit, Sam, not my — ah, my behind."

She looked at Anastasia, who had been watching the two of them in amazement. "*Sam* isn't afraid of me," she said. "Are you, Sam?"

Sam was busy folding an envelope he had found on Mrs. Bellingham's desk. "Nope," he said. "Because I love you."

"Mrs. Bellingham," said Anastasia, "Daphne loves you, too. I know she does. It's just that she's growing up. And it isn't *easy* to grow up. Life gets very complicated when you're thirteen."

"Yes," said Daphne's grandmother thoughtfully, "I guess that's true. Daphne and I will have to work things out. We'll have to talk.

"Anastasia," she added, "I haven't told your parents about last night. I had to tell Daphne's, I'm afraid. But I'll leave it to you to tell your own."

"I will," said Anastasia. When I'm thirty, she thought.

"Look!" said Sam suddenly. "I made a flypaper all by myself!" He launched the folded envelope and it sailed across the room, coming to rest on top of the set of Henry James.

"Anastasia," said Mrs. Bellingham, "that was your pay that just zoomed by your nose."

❀

Later that afternoon, while Sam was taking his nap, Daphne called.

"Anastasia," she said dramatically, "this is the last time you'll hear my voice until school starts next week."

"Why?"

"Because I'm practically in solitary confinement. I got permission to make one phone call — even criminals get to make one phone call before they go to prison.

But after this I'm restricted to the house. And no phone calls. No nothing, until school."

"Because of last night?"

"Of *course* because of last night. I practically ruined my grandmother's reputation and everything."

"But, Daphne," said Anastasia, "you told me that your parents were very forgiving. They let you do anything!"

"Yeah, that used to be true. But my father really blew his stack over this. They almost sent me off to reform school."

*"Reform school?"*

"Well, boarding school. Same thing. But I cried so much they changed their minds. And I said I was sorry, and promised to do well in school this year, and everything."

"Were you acting when you said it?" asked Anastasia.

Daphne hesitated, as if she was thinking. "Actually, no," she said finally. "I really was sorry. And I really do want to do well in school for a change. Trouble is, I'm not sure I remember how. I'm so used to making trouble."

"What happens if you get into more trouble?"

"Boarding school for sure." Daphne moaned. "Probably one with bars on the windows."

"Well, Daph," said Anastasia, "I'll tell you what. I'll be your watchdog when school starts. I'll keep reminding you all the time to stay out of trouble."

"You will? Promise?"

"Sure. And I'll bug you to join the Dramatic Club and to try out for plays, okay?"

"Okay. And, Anastasia . . ."

"What?"

"If I start thinking up sinister schemes or anything, *stop me*. Will you do that?"

Anastasia laughed. "Atcher service," she said.